THE VALENTINE DINE OR DIE

A MAC AND MILLIE MYSTERY

JB MICHAELS

HARRISON AND JAMES PUBLISHING

For Madison Paige

THE VALENTINE DINE OR DIE

By JB Michaels

CHAPTER ONE

The Tiny Wanderer stood strong against the bitter cold of February, which made the irony of the romantic seemingly warm, maybe even steamy holiday of Valentine's Day's placement in this winter month that much more poignant. Mac's leg ached more than usual in the subzero wind chill as he made his way from his car to the yellow awning of his favorite side entrance of the retail mansion.

He'd made considerable progress on his memoir of his heroic exploits stopping a bombing during the Chicago marathon. The excitement of having solved a murder during Geneva's Christmas Walk cleared his mind and perhaps temporarily quelled his natural urge to act the policemen. A job he sorely missed, though many say you never stop being a cop. You always notice things others don't. Have natural protective instincts, smarts, etc.

He made his way into the Tiny Wanderer.

"Horrendous out there today, Edith!" Mac walked past her opening her cash register in the lamp room of the Tiny Wanderer.

"Morning, Officer O'Malley. I know, it will probably be a slow day. Who wants to shop on a day like today?" Edith kept her focus on counting the singles for the cash register.

"You'd be surprised you will probably have a bunch of idiot husbands and boyfriends walking in here on their lunch looking for something for their wives for Valentine's Day." Mac stood in front of the counter Edith stood behind.

"This is true. And have you found anything yet for your dear Millie?"

"Ha! No, I have no idea what to do. I will figure something out."

"If you don't want to buy her a gift, you could take her to a show, you know." Edith closed the register and looked up at him.

"Oh, now there is a good idea. What ya thinking?"

"My son Billy is a server over at the Potter House and there is a special interactive dinner theater event there tonight. Ronnie and I were supposed to go, but of course he is sick with the flu. You can have our tickets if you want." Edith fished something from her purse on the back counter.

"Now that sounds like fun! Thanks so much, Edith."

Edith turned and handed two tickets to Mac.

"The Valentine Dine or Die! What a cool name! Ha! Love it! How much do I owe you?"

"Don't even worry about it. It is the least I could do for you after what you did during the Christmas Walk." Edith smiled.

"Edith, I was just doing my job. Well, my old job, but still. I will pay you for this somehow. You really bailed me out here. I was going to make chicken tonight with some candles at my place. This is way better. I can't wait to surprise Millie."

CHAPTER TWO

Millie settled into work. She took a sip of her hot green tea and logged into her computer at Geneva's Salem Bank and Trust. She had a fairly slow day ahead. Only one appointment scheduled so far. Walk-ins were indeed welcome on this horribly cold Valentine's Day. She could catch up on a few other paperwork items and the balance sheets for her top clients.

Patricia, the murdered owner of The Tiny Wanderer's will and testament had been read and the retail palace had been passed on to her daughter Susan. The paperwork was signed, sealed, and the monies and deeds transferred. That was the last big task she'd had since the holiday rush. The winter was just slow. Tax season kicked in, but Mille automated the 1099 forms a while back. She could double-check those, but they were never wrong.

Millie's boredom grew.

Her thoughts drifted to Mac, her love, and how well they worked together during the murder investigation. Also, just how gracefully Mac handled her witchy ways. He was ever curious and wanted to know more about her magical powers but wasn't pushy. Millie could sense he suppressed his need to know more. One day she may tell him everything about her family's history of magic but not quite yet. She didn't want to scare him away. Although he probably wouldn't leave. Their bond was too strong.

She smiled and opened her desk drawer. She'd made him a valentine card with an original poem that was more farcical than sappy-romantic. Millie did write greeting cards for a card company, yet she didn't tell anyone. A candlelit reading tonight at Mac's place would do. She wanted to read it aloud to him. She wanted to make sure the syntax was perfect.

"Millie, can you come into my office, please?" A voice sounded from behind.

Startled, Mille spat out her green tea onto her keyboard and some liquid spray pelted Mac's valentine. Crap.

"I didn't mean to startle you!" Millie's boss Gerald stood with his hands up.

"All good. All good. My fault. I scare easily. I will be right in. Um, just let me clean this... clean this up real quick, Mr. Salem. Be right there." Millie stood up and grabbed tissues from the end of her desk.

"Again, sorry." Gerald walked back into his office.

The paper valentine already started to bubble and distort. Maybe she would have time to replace it. What the hell did Gerald want anyway?

Millie composed herself, wiped her jacket sleeve, and entered the walled off corner lobby office of Gerald Salem, bank manager.

"Millie, have a seat." Gerald's bald head, bearded face, and thick glasses screamed officer manager.

"Thanks." Millie sat in the cushy cloth gray chair.

"Millie, as you know, you are an invaluable member of the Salem Bank family. I don't need to retread how great you are."

"By all means you can do that. I don't mind." Millie laughed.

Gerald laughed super loudly. So loud. Millie still grinned through her annoyance with him.

He took the thick glasses off and wiped a tear from his eye. "You are hilarious. Anyway, I wanted to offer you a district manager position in upstate New York. Triple your current salary. We have taken over a small bank there and we need someone to oversee all the branches."

Millie's eyes widened. Her mouth opened with a gasp.

CHAPTER THREE

Mac searched for "Valentine Dine or Die" on his Mac's web browser. The Potter House presented a unique one-night event with interactive storytelling. A whodunit for couples on Valentine's night in the spirit of classic murder mystery movies and movies.

"This is going to be so much fun!" Mac said aloud in the atrium café of the Tiny Wanderer.

The same crabby man who shared the same space as Mac every morning pounded a fist on his small table. Followed by the obligatory crumpling of his morning newspaper.

"I don't understand why we do this most mornings? Why can't we just be friends? I am excited about life. I don't need your permission." Mac stared at the cranky man.

Response the same as always. Paper back up. No verbal warnings just grunting and crumpling paper.

"Someday I will get through to you, Mister Crankypants." Mac pointed at him even if the old crank couldn't see the gesture.

He dove back into the description of his night ahead. He couldn't wait to tell Millie.

This would certainly cover the dinner aspect of his valentine for Millie. The actual gift he did have figured out but didn't want to tell Edith. Mac pulled a small manila envelope from his jacket pocket. Inside it—the key to his place.

Mac looked at his watch. He wanted to put a solid hour's worth of work before informing Millie of the new plan for this evening. Before he closed the browser, he looked at the requirements for the event. Tie and dress. That should be okay. Mac would just stop at home for lunch and get his suit ready.

Better call Millie now.

"Hello! Happy Valentine's Day," Millie said.

"Happy Valentine's Day, love! How are things going at the bank today?" Mac asked.

"Not much of anything actually. No customers. One appointment later that will probably be canceled because who wants to go out in the cold if they really don't have to. So yeah. How is the writing going?"

"It is not quite started yet. I have been distracted

by our dinner this evening." Mac's voice rose with excitement.

"Oh yeah, did you want me to bring anything? I could stop at the store before I come over after work."

"About that. I have arranged for a change of plans. Edith gave us tickets to a cool dinner theater event at the Potter House this evening. Would that be something you are interested in?"

"That sounds like fun actually. What is it exactly?"

"It is right up our alley. It's called 'The Valentine Dine or Die' interactive murder mystery. It is certainly expensive, but Edith's son is in the cast and comped her tickets, but now the tickets are ours! Should be a unique way to spend Valentine's Day dinner. We keeping them or do you want me to find another place for them?"

"No, no. Let's do it. What is the dress code?"

"Was just going to tell you. You may want to stop at home for a dress and I have to grab my suit and tie at lunchtime. I will come pick you up from your place at about six forty-five. See you then. Love you, Mills!"

"Love you too, Mac. See you then."

Mac ended the call and then cracked his knuckles and loudly cleared his throat. Then of course looked up at the crank. Nothing, no response this time. Just a flip of his newspaper page.

Back to writing his memoir.

CHAPTER FOUR

Millie sat at her desk and rubbed her forehead in one particular spot above her left eye. Gerald just offered her a huge promotion. A significant advancement for her career but in another state. And she was looking forward to a quiet dinner with Mac tonight and now they were going to some dinner theater event. She had to put more effort into her appearance and probably change her dress eight times before she settled on the dress she thought would work best.

Whatever.

It would be a fun night. Supposedly.

Then there was the problem of the ruined valentine for Mac. She opened the drawer again and looked at the damage. A few small bubbles on the red with gold lettering card. Should be fine. He wouldn't care.

He'd care about her possible move to upstate New York.

Millie didn't know if she wanted to take the job and she informed Gerald she would think about it and get back to him within the next couple days. Still, her entire life was here. Becca and Hank. Now Mac. Her brother and sister. Friends and extended fam. Of course, she worked very hard at the bank for years for an opportunity like this one. She just thought that the opportunity would be local and not hundreds of miles away.

Pain spiked behind her eye again. Stress induced headache. Not good.

Millie suffered from headaches and sometimes, the intense gauntlet of migraines. Examining computer screens all day did little to quell her ailment. This combined with her natural efficiency and inherent ability to maintain focus helped keep a steady daily headache. She sometimes wished to be more like Mac with his ability to lose focus frequently. Perhaps then her headaches would be more infrequent. But she also was not nearly as big of an idiot as Mac could be. So, headaches she could live with.

A dinner theater event was much different than a quiet evening dinner and the more she thought about it the more irritated she became. The pain spread from behind her eye and across her entire forehead. Sinus headache?

Becca suffered from the same cranial issues and concocted a potion that did help numb the hurting. Disruptus dolor or as Becca called it Dolores. Do you need Dolores today? A question that she always asked. Millie would refuse because Dolores made her loopy. Sometimes, Millie even forgot what happened the rest of the day if she took Dolores. She was always highly functional and never got into any car accidents. No one complained of erratic behavior. It was harmless except for the memory loss. It didn't always happen, and it may not happen, but you never know.

Still, the pain was bad. She could risk taking Dolores and have a pain-free pleasant first Valentine's Day with Mac but also not remember any of it. She opened the bottom file drawer of her desk and pulled out her purse.

Millie sighed as she unzipped her purse and read the label her mother wrote on the brown bottle 'Ditzy Dolores.' A laugh burst from Millie's mouth.

She grabbed 'Ditzy' and took a sip. Dolores did wear off in three to four hours. She would be fine. A sip would hopefully do enough to take the edge off. Maybe one more sip just to be safe.

CHAPTER FIVE

Mac felt confident in his day's work. A few more chapters and he could even send a draft to his editor in New York. Reliving the marathon day impacted Mac more than he let on. His leg hurt more during his written reenactment yet served as a reminder of the lives he saved. Better his leg than dozens of runners and bystanders along Lake Shore Drive.

"Okay, Edith. I am done for the day." Mac stood up and secured his cane to the floor.

"Seems like you were more focused today. Have fun tonight and let me know how the Dine or Die goes!" Edith waved.

"I will. Thanks again!" Mac walked through the linen department to the side door exit.

The sun's light faded. Dusk on full display. Mac

was excited to pick up Millie and head to the Potter House for a night of fun entertainment.

MILLIE MUST HAVE LOOKED in her full-length mirror eight times in various poses, positions, stances. The evening's bitter cold did help guide her to a high neckline. However, most of her dresses were cut with a plunging neckline, appropriate for warmer weather occasions. She had one red sweater dress that did complement her natural hair and skin color. That would have to do.

She looked at the time displayed on her phone. Mac would be here very soon.

Millie again resisted the urge to change into a different dress. All that was left to take care of was her lipstick. A bright red similar to the color of her outfit.

She applied the lipstick, shut her eyes, and did a pain gauge. Ditzy Dolores worked to ease her head pain, and she didn't think she would need more. She also could remember the rest of her workday, so that helped her maintain confidence that her first Valentine's dinner with Mac would be unaffected by her mother's crazy concoction.

The soft chime resounded in the hallway. Mac had arrived. Just need to put on shoes and a jacket.

The doorbell rang again. Mac wasn't exactly impatient, but his patience did wear thin at times.

"Be right there!" Mille opened her closet door and started throwing shoes around until she found a pair of black flats. She ran down the hallway to the door. Behind the door was Mac looking dapper as ever. A steel gray suit with a dark red tie draped over a textured white shirt.

"You look absolutely gorgeous, Millie!" Mac smiled.

"As if I don't look this way all the time. Ha! You aren't looking too shabby yourself there, Officer O'Malley."

"Oh, well, you know it's not every day you get to solve a murder in downtown Geneva looking this good." Mac leaned on his cane to walk in Millie's apartment.

"Speaking of which, how exactly will tonight work? Is this more a dinner show or a game show type thing?" Millie grabbed her jacket she'd draped over a dining room chair.

"We are about to find out." Mac helped Millie with her jacket and off they went.

CHAPTER SIX

The Potter House was built in 1857 by a lumber merchant for his family to reside in. Lumber being one of the five major businesses that drove people to the Chicagoland area. The construction looked similar to when it was first built as it had been restored by an entrepreneurial family looking to open a restaurant inside. The two-story red-brick house crowned by a circular window in the center just under the roof lay ahead. Mac and Millie made their way up the sidewalk. Mac had counted nine windows, five on the top floor and four on the bottom floor. Yellow light emanated from the inside, splashing a warm glow on the steps of the vast wooden wraparound porch.

A portable signpost warned possible customers of a special event for the evening and to come back for regular hours the next day.

"Let's do this, you sexy sleuth you." Mac laughed. He opened the door to the restaurant to be greeted by stairs to the top floor. To the right of the stairs the hostess stand. No hostess. A man dressed in a butler outfit stood behind the stand.

"Greetings. May I see your tickets for the evening's dying, I mean, dining?" The butler stood stone-faced.

"Ha! I see what you did there." Millie winked at the butler. No response. "Okay."

"I have the tickets. Here you go, sir." Mac spoke with his best English accent.

The butler examined the tickets and led them into the room right next to the main hallway. A beautiful red-brick fireplace crackled and there were only a few tables in the room with high back black wooden chairs. No one but Mac and Millie had arrived yet.

Stone-face the butler led them to a corner table that faced two front windows. He carefully pulled a chair out for Millie to sit in.

"Thank you." Millie sat down.

"I can get mine. Thanks." Mac nodded and pulled his own chair out. Stone-face had already walked away.

"Is it warm in here? Are you warm?" Millie asked.

"Yes, very warm. They have the fireplace going but also looks like an old radiator heat too." Mac pointed to a darkly painted radiator coils right under a window.

"That window is even open and it's still superhot

in here. I know I am not due for hot flashes quite yet." Millie waved her hand over her cheek.

"Interesting. So far not very impressed with the experience. The house itself is really cool, though. Oh, here come some more peeps."

An elderly couple walked in. Dressed to the nines. A mink coat for the woman and a Burberry trench coat for the man. They were seated almost directly in front of the fireplace. Stone-face took their jackets for them.

"He didn't take our jackets. What the heck?" Mac observed.

"Maybe we are in the cheap seats?" Millie shook her head.

"Perhaps he just forgot. Whatever. Here comes another couple. There are only two more tables in here. So just eight of us, which explains how expensive the tickets were. This must be quite the dining experience. Surprised we didn't have to sign some release." Mac rubbed his chin.

Two men sat at a table in front of the closed window on the other side of the fireplace. That left one more table nearest the radiator coils and the open window.

"We are the only people on this side of the fireplace. I wonder if something happens on this side of the room. Maybe this is where most of the action takes places. This table could be great, Mills!"

THE VALENTINE DINE OR DIE   19

"Mac. Shush. Look who it is." Millie pointed to the final couple that entered the room.

"Am I supposed to know these people?"

"That is the co-host of 'Good Morning USA' Rachel Waddle and her husband."

"Oh, that's right." Mac nodded.

"You have no idea who she is, do you? Mac, it's okay to admit you are a big idiot sometimes."

"Ha! You are right, I have no clue who she is."

"They tape the show in downtown Chicago. She lives out this way."

Rachel Waddle was dressed in a sparkly red dress akin to a '20s flapper with long black gloves. Her straight blond hair hit her shoulders and the possibility of Botox injections made her lips jut out a bit. Still, she was beautiful. Her demeanor cheerful. A perfect anchor for a morning TV series.

"How is she married to that guy?" Mac whispered.

The balding, husky husband of Rachel Waddle sat down in his chair in front of the radiator coils and open window. His broad shoulders denoted years of exercise that built solid muscle that now gave way to soft fatty tissue. Bags under his deep-set eyes. He just looked tired and unpleasant.

"Stop! He isn't so bad...I guess. Well, this ought to be an interesting evening. We are among celebrities that aren't hero cop Mac O'Malley. She would have probably interviewed you had they started the show before your heroics."

"This is true. I am sure her salary can easily pay for the tickets."

Stone-face the butler walked in and stood in front of the fireplace. "Ladies and gentlemen, welcome to the Potter House. I am Rutherford, this estates' resident butler. Dinner will be served shortly. Our staff will be out to take your order. Please enjoy this singular entertainment as it is our newest show but our best show. Thank you for choosing to die with—dine with us."

The small, intimate audience laughed.

CHAPTER SEVEN

Mac and Millie both ordered the sirloin steak. Mac sipped his craft beer, Millie her wine while they waited for more entertainment and their main course. Rutherford acknowledged the warmth of the room and moved the logs in the fireplace around to make the flames die out quicker. The chandelier hanging from the center above the older couple's table provided enough light to keep the room's mood romantic yet brightly lit.

Mac looked around the room then focused his attention on Rachel Waddle and her husband.

"Your favorite TV show host doesn't seem to be having much fun." Mac pointed a finger while sipping his beer.

"I noticed. Seems like she is trying to cheer him up. She is on her second glass of wine already." Millie raised both eyebrows.

"He is not having it. Oh, good, here comes our appetizer. I think our server may be Edith from the Tiny Wanderer's kid."

The server, a young man in his early twenties, perfectly coiffed hair, a full Windsor necktie, and white apron walked in with a basket of bread.

Suddenly the chandelier's lights went out.

There was some applause from somewhere in the room as whoever clapped must have thought the show was underway.

Visibility was extremely low. Darkness enveloped the room. Mac searched for Millie's hand.

A gunshot rang out. Loud. Powerful. Brief. The room's high ceilings made the noise that much louder.

A gasp.

A scream. Another blood-curdling scream. A guttural growl akin to Mac's favorite hard rock band, ACDC.

The volume pained Mac's ears.

The chandelier flashed then pulsed back to full power.

Rachel Waddle screamed.

"Somebody! Somebody, please help!" The morning show host stood up and pointed to her slumped husband. He slid off his chair and onto the ground.

"Mac, I don't think this is part of the show." Millie grabbed Mac's hand.

Mac stood. No cane necessary.

He looked at Rachel's husband on the floor.

Mac hobbled between the elderly couple and the fireplace to Rachel's husband.

Blood poured from a hole in the right side of his head. Powder burn ringed around the wound.

Real blood.

"Rutherford. Lock the doors and call the police."

CHAPTER EIGHT

"Mac. The gun. His right hand." Millie stood behind Mac and pointed.

Mac looked. The .38 caliber pistol was loosely held in his right hand. His index finger, however, was not in proximity to the trigger. The fall could have jostled the gun around. The shock of the bullet hitting his brain also could have caused a spasm in his arm. Brain injuries tend to send all sorts of strange signals throughout the human body, often causing strange spasms, etc. Mac couldn't be sure what exactly happened and why the gun moved the way it did in his hand.

The supposed hand that enacted suicide.

"Ladies and gentlemen, I am Mac O'Malley, retired cop and new Geneva resident. I need everyone to stay calm and to stay in the Potter House until the police arrive."

The abject shock that permeated the room kept everyone silent.

"This is most definitely not part of the dining experience we had planned for you. You will receive a full refund." Rutherford walked in. His proper English accent dropped for his Midwestern natural.

Mac felt a draft. He looked to the hallway. Vince, his detective brother, walked in the room. "Geneva PD. Everyone just stay calm. We will try and get you out of here within a reasonable time. Jesus Christ, Mac and Millie. What the hell are you doing here?"

"I swear we just wanted to enjoy a romantic dinner of theater and death...whoops," Mac said.

"Seriously, Mac. Not the time to joke." Millie shook her head.

Rachel Waddle let out a whimper and cry.

"I am just going to take her into another room." Millie put her hand on Rachel's shoulder. Rachel poured herself into Millie's arms. Millie helped her stand up and moved her out of the room.

"Nice to see you too, by the way, Vince. Possible suicide here. The placement of the gun in his hand bothers me, though. Doesn't seem quite right to me."

"We need to question the wife first and foremost. I got a few squads rolling up to keep everyone in the building until we can talk to everyone." Vince ran his fingers through his gray hair and sighed.

"I can help you with the questioning. His right side was against the radiator coils and the window. So, unless someone stood up when the lights were out and reached to his right side and popped him then put the gun in his hand. This is a suicide."

"Of course it's a damn suicide. We were all seated when the light went out!" the older man yelled.

"The lights went out?" Vince took out a small notepad from his peacoat.

"Sir, what's your name?" Mac asked.

"I am Roger Hern and this is my wife Edna." Roger put a hand on his wife's wrist. She seemed unaffected and handled it better than Roger.

"Roger, we will cooperate and leave here soon."

"Of course. Of course!" The distraught Mr. Hern was actually the one who needed comfort.

Vince signaled to Mac to join him in the hallway. They walked out of the dining room.

"What is going on here, Mac? Why are there only a few people in this restaurant on Valentine's Day?"

"I told you, dinner theater. Supposed to be a very expensive dinner and show experience. The Valentine Dine or Die. Edith from the Wanderer gave us the tickets. Her son is in the show and in here somewhere. I had no idea it would be this authentic."

"Mac, Millie's right. Stop making bad jokes."

"The jokes write themselves. For reals. Anyway, this doesn't seem to be a murder anyway. Seems like a clean suicide." Mac wished for his cane. His leg hurt from standing too much. He was hungry and he still wanted to give Millie the key to his place. He didn't envision his first Valentine's Day with Millie going this way.

"Look at you the eager beaver a couple months ago with the Christmas Walk killer and now you want to dismiss this as a suicide and leave. His wife was sitting right across from him. Let's properly investigate before we just dismiss everyone. You said yourself the gun seemed oddly positioned in his hand. Hey, butler kid, the four people can leave the room just not the restaurant. Got it? Also, clear the bar area. We will be doing interviews in there with each individual in this building."

CHAPTER NINE

Perry Schroeder, a wealthy contractor and builder of dream homes in the Fox River Valley lay dead on the floor of a historic house on 2nd street in Geneva, Illinois. An apparent suicide. Or perhaps not. The night's work would hopefully help Mac find out more about this man.

"Love you and your show. You say your husband was quite the successful builder. Did he have any reason to be upset over his business or work situation?" Mac asked, leaning on the bar.

"No, Perry loved his work. Nothing about work would cause him to do this. Thank you for watching." Rachel wiped the mascara that ran down her cheek still, even after Millie helped her compose herself in the bathroom. She sat on a barstool in the small room with a curved granite bar and an assortment of taps and hard liquor bottles along the wall.

"What about his mental state as of late? Has he been down at all?" Vince asked.

"He has been acting a bit strange as of late, but Perry did suffer from, what do they call it? The winter blues? You know the lack of sunlight thing. I took him out tonight to this event for a night of fun. I mean, he typically did struggle during winter in general. Work slows down for him. Not a ton of people break ground in the winter."

"Seasonal Affective Disorder is what it's called. Has there been any significant deaths in the family?" Vince asked. He held his notepad but looked intently into Rachel's eyes.

"No, no deaths in the family. He did lose his mother in the winter two years ago. He struggled with that from time to time, but that is normal." Rachel sighed.

"Rachel, did Perry drink or smoke a lot? Any vices we should know about?" Mac interjected.

"He liked to drink whiskey but not every night." Rachel rubbed the back of her neck.

"Rachel, did your husband have any enemies? Any unhappy customers?" Mac shifted his weight off the bar and put his weight on the cane.

Rachel paused.

Mac's and Vince's eyes met for a brief moment.

"Over a twenty-year career, Perry did have difficult customers from time to time. It comes with the territory. The older couple in the room, the Hern family. They were particularly difficult at times, I recall. When he saw them in the room, his mood took a turn for the worse."

"Was he in a bad mood already or just after he saw the Herns?" Vince asked.

"He was in a neutral mood, I suppose, but when he saw them...it changed." Rachel's eyes began to tear up once more. She took a deep breath and put her now ungloved hand on her chest. She regained her composure.

Mac noted the gloves. She had long black gloves on. Where did the gloves go?

"How bad did things get? Bad enough that they might murder him in cold blood and make it look like a suicide? Can you tell us anything about the exact moment the gun went off? Since you were so close it could help us understand what happened."

"No. I don't know. They don't seem like murderers, but how the hell would I know? I didn't think Gordon the realtor was a killer, but he was. It was pitch-black in the room. There was an orange flash where the gun went off and the loud noise of course. I went into shock and was overwhelmed at first. I struggled to catch my breath then finally screamed then called for help. Can I-I be excused for a moment?" Rachel put her hand over her mouth, denoting sickness. She shuffled back to the bathroom. Millie, who stood at the far end of the bar during the questioning, followed her in.

"Shall I get the Herns in here?" Mac asked.

"Yes, of course. May be a longer night than we think." Vince puffed his cheeks, blew air, and reviewed his notes.

CHAPTER TEN

Edna Hern sat in the barstool, cool as can be, not a nervous bone in her body. Mac was impressed. Everyone showed some nerves while being questioned by the police. Not Edna. Roger seemed much more worried about the events of the evening than his wife.

"Mrs. Hern, can I get you a drink of water?" Mac walked behind the bar to get himself a glass of water.

"No, I am not thirsty." Edna smiled then frowned, denoting her impatience.

"Mr. Perry Schroeder, did you know him?" Vince readied his pen to his notepad.

"I assume she already told you. Yes. We knew Perry. Perry was an asshole."

No sooner did Mac sip his newly poured glass of water, he swallowed wrong and coughed in response to Edna.

"Mrs. Hern, can you elaborate on your feelings about Perry?" Vince's eyes were wide.

"He built our house seventeen years ago. He didn't listen to our needs. They built our subdivision and they wanted to throw up the houses as quickly as they could. Needless to say, we had to have Halliburton come in and make the changes we needed after the house was completely built. He cost us a lot of money."

"Halliburton?" Vince asked.

"The other major housing contractor in the area." Edna rolled her eyes.

"Mrs. Hern, did you have any communication with Perry since your house was built?"

"Never. Officer O'Malley, I may have had no love for Mr. Schroeder, but I didn't kill him and make it look like he committed suicide and neither did my husband. I am leaving." Edna stood up and walked out of the room.

"Mrs. Hern! We aren't done. Your table was close enough to Rachel and Perry! Officer Jackson, don't let her leave this building. Also, Roger? Get him in here next." Vince followed her out of the bar area.

"Officer O'Malley, are the Herns being charged with anything? That answer I can tell you is no. They are leaving and leaving now." A raspy, female voice sounded from the hallway.

"Shit. Not Vergara." Vince shook his head. Mac

followed him into the hall where a raven-haired woman in a suit, probably forty-five years of age, stood with a briefcase.

"I assume that is the Herns' attorney," Mac said.

"Yes, yes, it is. She is very good at what she does, too."

"Oh man, this means that it isn't storming terribly outside? We aren't all locked in the house with a killer together and have a brilliant twisty reveal of the culprit in a couple hours?"

"Bro, you really have to stop with the movie references. We have others we can interview. Where is the other couple?"

"The Werners are waiting in the bar. They are willing to answer questions but are eager to leave," Rutherford informed from the dining room entryway.

"I should really interview them separately." Vince rubbed the back of his neck and walked back to the granite bar.

"Let's just get this over with. I think this may actually just be an unfortunate suicide, Vince." Mac smiled at the Werners upon reentering the bar.

Two men, one older with white hair and matching goatee. The other a few years younger with blond hair.

"I knew Perry. I knew Perry. He could be a jerk but ultimately, a good guy." The white-haired Werner had tears in his eyes on the verge of a panic attack.

"You knew Perry too?" Vince looked befuddled.

"Yes, I did help furnish and design the interiors of his model homes for a few years. He could be a stickler at times, but he was always fair, I feel. My name is Peter, by the way." Peter paced alongside the bar.

"So, you worked with the Schroeder company? Were you close with him?" Mac asked.

"No, we had a professional relationship. I did hear a rumor that he didn't have the best marriage. That was just talk amongst people who worked with him. He wasn't exactly rainbows and sunshine. People just figured things weren't good at home. Maybe they were right."

"Thank you for your statement, Peter. Have a safe drive home." Vince cut the interview short.

"If you need anything else please call us." Peter and his husband put their jackets on and left the bar.

"Why did you cut that short?" Mac resumed drinking his glass of water he'd left on the bar.

"He was in a bad marriage. Had a stressful job. Seasonal Affective Disorder. The guy wasn't well. He probably did end his life. It still just bothers me that the lights happened to go out. Was that part of the dinner show?"

"If I may interject. Yes, Officer, with the presentation of the bread service, the lights were supposed to go out and one of our servers who was an actor was meant to fall on the floor and act the victim." Rutherford hovered once more.

"Perry just happened to time his suicide perfectly. Took advantage of the theatrics." Mac nodded.

"Well, we shall see what the examiner says about the body. Right now, it seems pretty cut and dry." Vince reviewed his notes.

"Can Millie and I leave now? Is she still in the bathroom with Rachel?" Mac asked.

CHAPTER ELEVEN

Rachel walked out of the bathroom first, followed closely by Millie.

"Rachel, do you need a ride home? One of my guys can you give you a ride," Vince said.

"I can drive home. It's fine. Is Perry still here?" Her composure regained. Her makeup removed. Hair up.

"He is still here and hasn't moved. The forensics team is here taking pictures. I want to make sure we determine exactly what happened. Due diligence. We will call you with any developments after the examiner takes a look at him," Vince said.

"Please keep me updated. Thank you, Officer." Rachel walked to Rutherford, who waited with her jacket ready. She left the Potter House.

Millie looked at Mac. "This has been a very strange night. Ready to go?"

"Yes, let's get the hell out of here. Maybe we can grab a burger from Stockholmen's."

"Let's just go through a drive thru." Millie stood with her hands on her hips. Exhausted. Hungry. Disappointed and distraught from the impending conversation about her promotion with Mac but also the night's unfortunate event.

Mac loosened his tie. "Vincey, you sure you don't want our help here?"

"No, you two try to have a good night. I will mop up here, interview the staff, and if anything develops, I will let you know. Go. Get out, you two lovebirds." Vince shooed them both out of the bar room.

"Did you get your wife anything?" Mac looked back at his brother.

"No. I am a little busy. Leave me alone. But it will be way better than the disastrous gift you got Millie this awful Dine or Die. Go." Vince laughed.

Millie laughed. She really liked Vince. He was less manic than his brother and more relaxed like herself.

"We are outta here." Mac walked into the dining room and grabbed their jackets. The forensics team were combing the room. Taking pics, measurements, marking spots, etc.

"Trouble seems to find us, Mr. O'Malley." Millie accepted Mac's offer to help her with her jacket.

"That it does. Well, things certainly don't get

boring with us! Always something! Good night, guys."
Mac waved at the members of the GPD.

"Good night, Mac," Officer Jackson responded.

Millie walked to the front door. The cold pene-
trated through the closed door. She didn't want to go
out in the cold. Geneva winters sucked. She loathed
living in the frozen Midwest. New York wouldn't be
much better as it was practically on the exact same
latitude.

She opened the door for Mac. They exited the
historic Potter House having solved no murders or
suicides, real or purely theatrical.

"I really need to get a remote start installed. This is
ridiculous. Why do we live here?" Mac shivered.

Perfect time to say something about the
opportunity.

"I know, right? I am so hungry and frankly freaked
out. I have never been a part of something like this."
Millie held hands with Mac as they walked to Mac's
car. Chickened out and frankly, not even sure what
to say.

"Well, you handled Jerry and Gordon well."

"Yes, but I didn't see Patricia's dead body, nor did
she lose her life right in front of me like Perry. That
poor man."

Mac opened the car door for her. She entered the
car and blew warm breath into her hands.

Mac hopped, well, hobbled in, threw his cane in the backseat, and started the car.

"I meant to ask you. How was Rachel in the bathroom? You two were in there a long time," Mac asked.

"What? The bathroom?" Millie stared ahead into the dark February night only lit by the headlights.

"Yes, you and Rachel were in there a couple times. She was pretty upset. What did she do with her black gloves? I noticed she didn't have them on when she came out for questioning."

"I have no idea what you are talking about. I am sorry." Millie felt a headache forming above her right eye.

"Millie." Mac pulled the car to the side of the road on a normally lit Rt. 38.

"Mac, I seriously can't remember." Millie rubbed her head and then realized the cause of her memory loss. She fished the small bottle from her purse. Dolores. Ditzy Dolores. Of all nights for this to happen.

"Millie, are you okay?"

"This. I took this concoction my mom makes to ease our headaches we almost always get. We call it Ditzy Dolores because it can cause loopiness and memory loss." Millie showed Mac the bottle.

"Dolores made you forget the whole time with Rachel in the bathroom? I mean, it's probably not a big deal. Let's hope not. What do you remember from tonight? Perry Schroeder died, Rachel's husband. You do remember that?"

"Yes, Mac. Yes. I remember that. I don't know why Ditzy causes me selective memory loss. I remember everything else."

"What about her gloves? Do you remember what she did with those?"

"Mac. Stop. I don't remember that either, okay? Can we get some food now, please?" Millie's patience with his hyped questioning wore thin.

"Okay, you are right. It's just that if she fired the gun there would be residue on the gloves is all. Just thought it was peculi—"

"Mac. Stop." Millie, for the first time ever, found herself irritated with him.

"I will just call Vince and tell him to do a sweep of the women's bathroom for the gloves. Sorry."

Millie needed food. Hunger didn't help her mood. She also felt terrible for not remembering and Mac's questions made her feel worse.

CHAPTER TWELVE

Mac woke up to the buzz of his phone's vibration function. Vince.

"Rise and shine, Mac attack, and meet me at the Riverside apartments next to the Hennington."

"Why are you calling me so early? Are we having breakfast?" Mac lifted himself off the couch and winced. His leg's usual morning aches always assured him he was to live another day.

"Just get down here." Vince ended the call.

Mac could hear the shower running down the hallway of his condo. Mac didn't feel great about what happened last night. The newish couple had had their first tense moment. Mac wouldn't really call it a fight, but it certainly wasn't pleasant. He couldn't let it go that she couldn't remember and was upset that she didn't just take an ibuprofen. Millie then fired back that it didn't work, etc. Just a dumb spat.

He realized that he made her feel worse for forgetting things that happened at the Potter House. The details would be smoothed over. Vince just called. Maybe he knew more. The examiner's report was probably complete.

It was rather dumb. Mac felt the manila envelope that was still stuffed in his pocket. The key to his place. It wasn't the right time. He walked to the bathroom door and knocked.

"Hang on. I am done," Millie yelled through the door.

The sound of the shower ceased.

"Okay, sounds good."

Millie opened the door. Her hair in scraggly wet curls. A towel around her body. She looked refreshed. Beautiful. Mac took a deep breath and smiled. He could get used to seeing her every morning.

"Vince called and asked me to go with him to the Riverside apartments. I am going to head out and I just wanted to say I am sorry again. I need to back off on being so demanding and critical of your headache remedies."

"It's fine. I shouldn't have been so irritated. It's just the questions just made me feel worse. I feel terrible that I can't remember some things from last night. I took the risk of taking Dolores because I just wanted our first Valentine's together to be headache-free and of course it backfired. Terrible choice of words. I should have said failed. Ha."

"It's okay. I made some terrible jokes last night that I hope you forgot. I'd better get going. Have a good day at work. It's Saturday and only for a few hours." Mac leaned in and gave her a kiss on the cheek.

"Yes, keep me updated on what Vince says!"

"Of course, I should probably brush my teeth or something. Ah, screw it."

"Gross, Mac."

"I am out!" Mac, still in his outfit from last night, grabbed his jacket and cane and walked out of the condo.

THE DRIVE to the Riverside apartments spurred Mac's usual review of key events from last night. Perry Schroeder committed suicide. That was the current working conclusion. The fact Vince called him cast doubt on that explanation. A .38 caliber Smith and Wesson fired in the dark in a small dining room in a historic house at the very same time the lights were to go out for the dinner theater made for impeccable timing on Perry's part. Would a downtrodden and unstable person time his death with the lights going off? Or did he reach for the gun and pull it up to the side of his head before the lights went out? Rachel made no mention of that at all. No shuffling sounds. Just her morose husband was alive seconds before as the chandelier was lit. *Lights go out. Bang! Lights go on. Husband is slumped in his chair with a bullet in his head and a gun loosely positioned in his right hand. Then he falls to the ground.*

All the while Rachel screamed at least twice.

Mac walked over and quickly assessed the situation and then called the person he drove up to in the parking lot of the Riverside apartments. The Fox River had a nice sheen of ice reaching out from the river-banks. The bright morning sun showed Vince had large bags under his eyes with a grande coffee from Starbrick's in his hand. He noticed his brother rub the sleep from his eyes.

"What we got, Vincey?" Mac pulled up next him and exited his car.

"Another dead guy." Vince nodded toward a brown Crown Victoria sedan that was only a few feet from plunging into the icy Fox River if it weren't for a tree that helped crumple the car's large front end.

"Another one! Two in less than twelve hours. What is happening? Time of death?"

"We think not long after Perry Schroeder died." Vince walked next to Mac.

Mac walked closer to the car. Blood splatter all over the dash, the passenger seat, and the passenger window. The victim had a brown jacket. Heavyset fella. Big head with a big hole in the side of it. The window was down. The driver window was down as this man must have been a smoker. Had the window down when the bullet hit the side of his head. Considerable caliber bullet made the side of his head a bloody mess. His hands were still on the wheel. The radio played in the car. Morning traffic updates.

"We think someone who could shoot a rifle from considerable distance away took the shot and nailed him on the first try. No other bullet holes anywhere around." Vince took a sip of his coffee.

"Why is the car wrapped around this tree trunk? He tried to get away?" Mac asked with a strong lean on his cane, still examining the car.

"Yep, he probably saw whoever held the rifle and tried to drive away," Vince said.

"The tire treads on this Crown Vic are non-existent. This icy parking lot didn't help him get away. We have a name for this poor guy?"

"Yes, one Devlin Hanks. An Aurora resident. No priors. A few tickets here and there. Guy works for the

Kane County Cougars Stadium. He ran the vendors there in the spring and summertime."

"What does he do in the off-season that would get him killed?" Mac rubbed his stubbly chin.

"A Hennington Inn maid called it in. She saw the car from a room she was cleaning. We are still working on his off-season occupations or lack thereof."

"Drug deal?" Mac opened the back door.

"No drugs. Nothing. We did a search of the car. Found his smartphone, but we can't get into it. We would know more if we could get into his phone."

"What about the gunshot? Anyone at the Henningon or the Riverside apartments hear a gunshot?" Mac held the back door open and looked inside the car anyway.

"No. No one heard a thing. No calls last night or any disturbance issues at all. Must have been a silenced shot."

"Wow. This is something else. Talking about some professional shit here, Vincey. Why was Mr. Hanks hunted down by a trained marksman? Does he somehow connect to Perry?"

"Well, that is the next thing I was going to tell you. Perry most likely didn't commit suicide. There was no residue on his right hand. The hand that loosely held the gun. .38s always leave residue." Vince took another sip of his delectable hot beverage.

"Oh shit. Rachel's gloves. Did you find any gloves in the bathroom after I called you last night?"

"No, we didn't find any gloves."

"Bring Rachel back in for questioning and demand the gloves."

"You were with me in the room when I questioned her, Mac. She wasn't lying and was visibly upset. Let's focus on Devlin and like you said see if there is any connection to him. I did a thorough investigation after you left. Questioned the rest of the staff and cast and all checked out. Someone murdered Perry, but we have no evidence to prove he didn't commit suicide yet."

"The lack of residue isn't enough?"

"No, Mac. It's not. It could have rubbed off as he fell—it's not enough. Besides it's better that people think we are chalking up Perry's death to suicide anyway and keep looking into it."

"I will have Millie look into some things. I will head to Aurora. Hanks have any family there? A roommate or girlfriend?"

"He lives with his mother in North Aurora near Orchard Rd," Officer Jackson chimed in from behind them.

"I am off. I got this. You guys keep up the good work at the scenes." Mac hobbled back to his car, carefully as to not slip on the icy lot.

"Mac. Thanks for the help, even though you should be writing your damn book!" Vince yelled.

Mac wanted to raise his middle finger but took his phone out instead. He had a hunch and Millie could help.

CHAPTER THIRTEEN

Millie settled into work at her desk. She probably should have spent a bit more time drying her hair as she swore parts of her hair were frozen. She turned on the computer. Some loan-processing had to be done this morning for close next week. Saturday mornings were usually relaxed. Although many people did get paid on the fifteenth of every month, so the bank could be busy in a little while.

Her phone buzzed in the drawer. Mac.

"Hey, Mills, you at work?"

"Yep, that is the current situation. What's up?"

Mr. Salem walked up to her desk. "Think about the offer some more?"

Millie panicked and dropped her phone. "Um, still giving it some thought. Thanks."

"Let me know soon, Millie. Please. You are the

right person for the job." Her boss walked away and into his office.

Millie picked her phone back up. She desperately wished Mac hadn't heard anything. Or did she? Maybe having the cat out of the bag would just help the dreaded conversation along.

"Hello? I dropped the phone." She laughed.

"No worries. Did Perry Schroeder bank with you guys?"

"Yes, I think so. He is one of the bigger accounts like Patricia was. Why? Need me to look something up?" Mille smiled. Mac was oblivious. Her phone drop worked.

"Just look and see if anything new was happening over the last couple months or so."

"Okay, why? What happened with Vince?"

"Another dead body. Time of death right around Perry's death. I am headed to Aurora to talk to the new vic's mother. We don't know what the guy did in the winter for a job. He worked for the Cougars in the summer. We just don't know much about the guy. Headed out to find out more."

"The plot thickens. Okay, I will get back to you soon. Love you. Keep me updated." Millie typed Perry's name into the client search field.

"Will do. Love you too." Mac ended the call.

Millie examined the checking account of one Mr.

Perry Schroeder. Builder extraordinaire. He didn't use his bank card very often. She started her search in November. Some bills to other banks, probably credit card payments for travel points. In early December, he withdrew $500 cash. Another $750 in later December, but that could be chalked up to the holidays, Millie assumed, but the credit card payments also went up in January. He could have paid for the gifts with his card. Another $2000 cash withdrawal in early January. Why all the cash?

Also, not particularly large sums relative to the amount of money Perry had just sitting in his bank accounts. What could he be using the money for? And why?

A customer walked in. One of her regulars. She would have to call Mac back in a bit.

CHAPTER FOURTEEN

Mac drove to 219 BriarCliff Rd. in the townhomes off Orchard Rd about fifteen minutes outside of Geneva in North Aurora, IL.

The homes were nice, samey, probably built in the early 2000s. They looked like white row houses in a suburb of London to Mac. One must pay attention to the numbers because you can easily get lost in a sub-divisional labyrinth such as this.

"219. 219. There it is." Mac parked his car in front of the Hanks household. He felt a pit in his stomach. Did Vince inform her that her son had died yet? Mac pulled out his phone and called Vince.

"Hello, Mac. Didn't think I would hear from you so soon."

"Did you tell this woman that her son has passed

away yet? I hate having to do this part of the job. I am not actually even on the job anymore." Mac sighed.

"She already knows. I understand. I made the phone call already. No worries. See what you can find out."

"Okay. Okay. Thanks." Mac sighed again. The job didn't always involve the intellectual stimulation of combing crime scenes for clues, the thrill of finding the culprit, and the sense of satisfaction when closing a case. The emotional toll weighed heavily at times. The victims had families, friends, a life lived before death's arrival.

Still, he needed more information on Devlin. This was the only way to find out. He would bring Devlin's murderer to justice.

He grabbed his cane and walked to the door of 219.

He knocked on the plain white door.

Mac's heart did pound a bit harder. Nerves still rattled his disposition. *Pull it together.*

The former cop knocked once more.

The door opened. A woman with salt and pepper hair and thick full-frame glasses stood in the doorway. "May I help you?"

Mac pulled out his retired badge. "I just have a few questions about your son, Devlin. I am sorry for your loss."

"Thank you. What do you need to know?"

Mac could smell the cigarette smoke waft from the house. He apparently would not be welcomed into this house.

"We know that Devlin worked at Cougar stadium in the summer. What does he do the rest of the year? We are just trying to find out as much as we can about your son."

"He helps me clean the townhomes. He was a good kid and wouldn't have gotten himself into any trouble. Leave me be. I told the GPD everything I knew."

"Ms. Hanks. Please. Can I come in?"

"No. No, thank you. I have much to do. Have a good day." Devlin's mom shut the door in Mac's face.

Mac's eyes went wide. What in the hell did Mrs. Hanks have to hide?

Mac would wait in the neighborhood awhile and see if she left the house. If she wouldn't talk, he would have to get in the house and see what he could find out about Devlin Hanks. With or without his mother's permission. Trusty lock picks at the ready.

CHAPTER FIFTEEN

Mac didn't have to wait long for Mrs. Hanks to leave the house. Fifteen minutes and she pulled her Buick LeSabre out of the garage. She probably had much to tend to. Considering her son was just murdered, she could be on her way to identify him for official purposes. Whatever the reason, it was time for Mac to see what he could find out about the Hanks family.

Before Mac left the car, he flipped his cane over and unscrewed the bottom rubber stopper and out fell his lucky lock picks. Not sure why he referred to them as lucky. The last time he'd used them he almost got caught by Gordon in his murdered mother-in-law's house. Still, he liked to use them and since he wasn't officially a cop anymore, he felt firmly justified in the ethical use of said lock-breaking devices. He screwed the bottom back on his cane and left the car.

To the plain white door, he went. Mac's heart raced. He felt partially naughty but also giddy to be on a case, searching for answers. Of course, Millie could probably conjure some magic spell that opened doors with a flick of her wand. That was no fun. He still couldn't quite wrap his head around that situation. Millie didn't really want to talk about it much. He respected her wishes as much as he could.

He reached the door and felt the cold metal of the lock picks in his bare hands. He touched the door handle. The door creaked open. Mac stood back then looked at the street for any sign of Mrs. Hanks and then naturally, let himself in.

Of course, someone else could be in the house. He listened. Silence. Not a creature was stirring, not even a mouse. The heat kicked on audibly from the furnace in the basement. That was it. No other indication that someone was home. Fortune favors the bold. Now where was Devlin's room? There was a staircase that led to the second floor bedrooms directly to his right and of course, the basement. A grown man might actually live in his mother's basement as a quasi-apartment. A somewhat independent living situation with a big emphasis on somewhat. He still lived with his mommy. Mac left his parents' house right after high school. Never understood how grown men couldn't leave the nest.

The basement first. Mac walked around the staircase to the kitchen and took a left into the kitchen.
There was a kitchen table and another hallway with a
door at the end. Garage entry most likely. Another
door opposite the kitchen table to the right. Must be
the basement entry. Mac put the lock picks in his
pocket and walked to the door.

There were many stairs, but the floor was carpeted
the whole way. The basement was furnished and
finished. Crème berber carpet. A bar area on the left
wall and sure enough an unmade bed on the right wall,
with a Star Wars comforter. Mac shook his head. A
man-child Devlin Hanks indeed was, unless he had a
brother or something. He looked around for any clues
this was Devlin's quarters. He walked over to a sofa
table in the middle of the room nestled behind the
couch in front of the big screen TV. Not a thin one,
though. An old DLP TV. A giant black box. In front of
the couch was a coffee table filled with gaming
controllers and discs. Also, a stack of Magnum PI
DVDs.

"Magnum? I love Magnum!" Mac yelled. He
couldn't contain his excitement. The full mustached,
slender yet muscular, Tom Selleck provided Mac with
hours of entertainment. Yet, that wasn't the only set of
physical media dedicated to crime-solving. James
Garner's Rockford Files. Murder She Wrote. Devlin

was obsessed with murder-mysteries and then he examined the couch. There was a crumpled piece of paper amongst other junk food wrappers. Mac picked up and smoothed out the paper. It was a half-filled out application to become a private investigator. Devlin Hanks was letting his love of Magnum PI influence his reality. He wanted to become a private investigator! Maybe he was on a case when he was killed? Devlin had no criminal record of any kind. What else would put him in such a precarious situation?

Mac quickly turned all the lights on in the basement and started snapping pics of everything with his phone. Maybe he would be able to find some clue as to who he may have been working for. Maybe even a connection to one Mr. Perry Schroeder. Still, getting into Devlin's phone would be his best bet at figuring out who could have hired him. If anyone did at all.

The screen of Mac's phone turned from a digital reflection of what lay in front of him in a physical space to the smiling emoji of his love, Millie.

"Hello, Mills, what you got?"

"Loo—recor—sum of—"

"Hang on, Millie, let me get out of the basement I am in. Signal is not good down here. Hang on." Mac walked up the stairs, holding his phone out in front of his face.

He reached the summit of the stairwell and entered the kitchen.

"Millie, you can talk now. I should have a better signal up..." Mac looked to his right. A large man dressed in a black heavy metal band T-shirt stood with the refrigerator door open. He looked up at Mac. His face flushed with fear and hopefully not, but probably anger. He slammed the door shut.

"Who the hell are you? Are you a cop?"

"Mills, call ya back." Mac's heart felt like it skipped at least six beats. He probably should have died right there on the kitchen floor.

CHAPTER SIXTEEN

The large man, possibly Devin's brother, cousin, lover, who knows? The man ran out of the kitchen and to the front door. Mac hobbled to catch up and risked the temporary excessive leg pain that came with fast movement and just held his cane and limped as fast as he could to catch the runner, well, more of a bounder. He wore black jean shorts in the middle of winter and his calves were muscular and gigantic from years of hauling around the extra weight.

"I might actually be able to catch up to this guy," Mac said in a low volume.

"Please just let me go!" the big fella yelled as he made his way outside to the icy street.

"Stop! Running! Why are you even running? Shouldn't I be the one running? Can we talk? Do you know Devlin Hanks?" Mac pushed through the front door and to the outside. He observed the heavy metal fan's glacial pace over a sheet of ice that formed on the street.

"Devlin?" He stopped. His large body mass went horizontal over the street and he fell directly onto his back, just like a Looney Tunes character. He lay still.

"Shit. You okay?" Mac carefully yet quickly used his cane to reach the street and leaned over the large man struggling to catch his breath. Then the sweet smell of marijuana drifted into Mac's nose. The big man flew so high off the ground because his disposition was that of a kite's on a blustery spring day.

Cannabis-induced paranoia caused the panicked run.

"You mentioned Devlin. He's my brother. Please don't arrest me." He looked up at Mac from the street.

Mac pulled out his retired badge and waved it above his head.

"You are a cop! I knew it! Please, I just like to download music and movies from the Internet, which I know is wrong! I am harmless!"

"I promise not to arrest you. Need a hand? What's your name?" Mac gripped his cane and held out his hand.

"No, no. I got it. I am Mikey. What happened—to Devlin?" Devlin's brother rolled to his stomach and lifted himself off the ice.

His mother hadn't communicated Devlin's death to his brother? Oh crap.

"We'd better get back inside. It's freezing." Mac patted the big man's back.

"You are right." Mikey walked ahead, plunging his hands into his armpits for warmth.

"I have to make a phone call. Be right in." Mac pulled out his phone to call Millie back. Anything to delay having to tell Mikey that Devlin was murdered.

"Hello, sir. Everything okay?" Millie's voice comforted.

"All is well, what you got for me?" Mac asked.

"Perry took out some cash in increasing increments from December into January. Not really sure why or if it even means anything, but still it could be something."

"I think I may know what the cash was used for. This may sound totally nuts, but what if Perry hired a private investigator? I am close to confirming the second body found was an amateur PI. I don't have any hard evidence yet, but I think I have some. I just need to get the victim's phone unlocked. Ugh." Mac's sigh signaled turmoil.

"Okay, let me know if you need any more help. You sure you are okay?" Millie asked again. Her concern grew.

"The second victim's brother is here, and I just

hate having to tell family members about a relative's murder. It is the worst."

"I can't imagine how hard that must be, but you really should tell him as soon as possible, Mac. You can do this," Millie assured.

"You are right. I have to do it. Okay, I will talk to you later."

"Just a second, I am very happy that I have someone with as big of a heart as you do, Officer O'Malley. Love you."

"Thanks, Millie. That means a lot. Love you too." Mac ended the call. He looked to the open plain white door of 219 BriarCliff Rd and took a deep breath.

CHAPTER SEVENTEEN

Mac gripped the handle of his cane and looked down at the salt-stained sidewalk. Millie was right. He had to tell him. He made his way to the door. He'd done it many times before. The weight of news like that of death had no equal. It hit hard.

He opened the door and walked into the front hall.

"I am in here, Officer. What is going on with Dev?" Mikey yelled from the kitchen.

Mac entered the kitchen to see Mikey sitting at the table with three different bags of chips open. He ate from all three in a pile on the table.

"I am surprised your mother hasn't told you. Your brother Devlin was murdered this morning and I was here trying to find out as much as I could about it. I shouldn't have just entered the house without permission. The door was open."

Mikey stopped eating and just stared at Mac.

"I am sorry for your loss. I just want to find the person who did this to your brother and I could just leave you my phone number if you want me to give you some time before I ask any questions."

The big brother wiped his hands on his shirt then held his face in his palms. His shoulders shrugged up and down several times over. He wept in front of Mac's eyes. Mac turned around. "I will be in touch, Mikey. Again, sorry for your loss."

"No, no. Wait. What information do you need from me?" Mikey coughed to clear his throat.

"First and foremost, what did your brother do the rest of the year in the offseason? Anything that might get him in some trouble like this?" Mac sat down at the table.

"How did you know he worked at Cougar stadium? Whatever. Doesn't matter. He worked with Mom at our small roadside diner in St. Charles. We own it." Mikey rubbed his eyes.

"Did you know that he wanted to be a private investigator? I saw an unfinished application for a permit downstairs."

"Yes, I helped him with his website and every-thing, but he said he didn't have any clients yet or clearance to even start investigating anyone. He said he was going to wait until spring to get things going there. So, my guess is he started and didn't tell anyone."

"He never told you he had any clients?" Mac leaned forward.

"No, he didn't. He was just gathering materials and tools of the trade."

"What tools of the trade?"

"You know surveillance equipment, a camera, a microphone, and a new laptop. I am not sure where he got the money, to be honest. I was a bit surprised when I went with him to the store and he pulled out cash."

"He paid cash? For everything?"

"He did. When I asked him about the cash, he told me not to worry about it and I was high at the time and didn't think anything of it."

"He ever mention a Perry Schroeder at all? Ever?"

"The Schroeders have a permanent skybox at Cougar stadium. We know them because we always bring food to them during games. Why?" Mikey's voice became more serious in tone with each question.

"Perry also died last night. There could be a connection between their deaths." Mac felt like he was getting somewhere.

"Oh man, that sucks. Loved Perry. He had a good sense of humor and always tipped us well. We knew them in a very casual manner. Devlin wasn't exactly close with them. I mean that I know of."

"Thank you so much for your time. You wouldn't happen to know your brother's passcode into his phone, do you? That could really help us."

"I do. Actually. It's 0988. Please keep in touch and let me know if you need any more help. Thank you, Officer O'Malley." Mikey walked over to Mac and gave him a bear hug.

Mac felt happy to have received a hug from Mikey. He patted his back. They both could have used a hug in that moment.

"You can thank me when we find out who did this to your brother."

CHAPTER EIGHTEEN

Mac made his way back to Geneva on Randall Rd. His excitement palpable. He gripped the wheel of his blue Chevy sedan. He called Vince.

"Hello, Macadamia Nut. How did it go in Aurora?" Vince's voice sounded tired. Deeper than usual.

"We are getting somewhere. I talked to Devlin's brother. His mother didn't want to answer any questions." Mac shouldn't have been holding the phone to his ear while driving, but he did anyway.

"Yeah, she was very tight-lipped with us too. Not really that emotional either. Sort of odd, but it happens. What did the brother have to say?"

"Well, there is a connection to one Perry Schroeder. The Hanks family catered Perry's food in his skybox at Cougar stadium. Also, Devlin had every intention of becoming a private investigator!"

"Mac. I mean, that is great and all, but what does that prove?"

Mac envisioned his brother shaking his head at him.

"Now wait a minute, maybe Perry hired him to do some work for him. They both suffered gunshot wounds to the head on the same night less than an hour apart. Also, now you can see for yourself. I have the passcode for Devlin's phone!"

"Mac, why didn't you lead with that? Give it to me."

"It's 0988. It should open right up."

"Hold up, it is just charging now. It was dead in the car. I will try turning it on."

"Where are you?" Mac drove closer to Geneva, passing the movie theaters in Batavia.

"I am at the station. I should be at home sleeping. Okay, booting the phone up now...uh-oh."

"What? What is happening? You just hold the side butt—"

"Mac! I know how to turn on a damn phone! I am not an idiot. The phone is brand-new or has been completely wiped. It's giving me the setup screen. I didn't even need the passcode."

"No! Oh man. Shit!" Mac pounded the steering wheel.

"Brother, just calm down. Don't even worry about

this anymore. I will handle it from here. Thanks for your help. Haven't you got some writing to do anyway? Head to the Wanderer. Get some coffee and chill."

"Yeah, like that is gonna happen." Mac shook his head.

"Mac, it's okay. I got this. Talk you later. Gotta go." Vince ended the call.

The rollercoaster of emotions Mac allowed himself to ride just came to an abrupt stop. The momentum he felt just moments before now swung in the other direction. The unknown murderer's direction. Maybe there was really no connection between Perry and Devlin other than passing acquaintance at the ballpark in summer.

Vince was right to suggest Mac head back to the Wanderer. Mac didn't want to write, though, he wanted to look at the photos in Devlin's basement. Maybe there was something in the pics to help and maybe there was some other lead he could mine from last night's interrogations. This wasn't over.

CHAPTER NINETEEN

Mac decided to change it up and walk to the front entrance of The Tiny Wanderer. He was correctly informed that the white colonial house exterior of the Wanderer was of Italianate architecture and not simply a colonial and that he should stop telling people it was merely colonial. Mac smirked and shrugged as he walked up to his favorite spot in downtown Geneva, IL. He made his way up the wooden steps to the covered porch and double door entrance. He walked in and was immediately met with the Valentine decorations adorning the staircase to the top floor. A silhouette of cupid hung from the stairwell. Wind from the open door made the nymph's arrow point straight at Mac.

Mac cocked his head. "Easy there, Cupid." The

events of the last twenty-four hours or so made the usual positive concept of being struck by Cupid's arrow rather negative. Two dead bodies and no solid leads made Mac a dull boy. Luckily, he had his Macbook and pictures to examine.

"Good Morning, Mac. How was your Valentine's Day?" Ann, from the purses and bags department, said.

"It was interesting to say the least. Could have been better." Mac wondered if the news had gotten out yet. In the age of information, a high profile death like Perry's should have gotten out, especially since Perry was married to Rachel Waddle, an American sweetheart who brought the news to Americans each morning. Maybe Vince was able to keep a lid on it. Mac envisioned a teary Rachel Waddle eulogizing her mentally ill husband on television.

"Okay, well, have a good day then. Headed to the café?" Ann asked.

"Yep, lots of work to do."

"Don't work too hard. It's Saturday!" She smiled as she removed the paper stuffing from a new Vera Bailey backpack.

"You too!" Mac smiled and adjusted his backpack strap and made his way down into the Atrium café. The white painted cast-iron rails and small tables comforted Mac. His grumpy friend must not come in on Saturdays. The place was empty. He loved it. He picked a spot in the corner with his back against the wall to keep a great view of his surroundings.

Juan walked up with a pot of coffee. "Good morning, Mac. Coffee?"

"You know it, buddy, thanks. Just the usual except add a couple pancakes. I am hungry this morning. Edith in?"

"She is off on Saturday mornings. Food will be right up." Juan smiled and walked to the kitchen area.

Mac opened the aluminum cover of his MacBook then popped in the USB cord from his phone to his laptop. He synchronized the pics from his phone over to the vibrant screen.

The pictures were darker than he had hoped. He clicked through. The man-child cave of Devlin's basement apartment at his mother's house displayed a charming arrested development. It belied an innocent naivete that watching the tidy plots and risk-averse-to-actual-danger crime television shows would inspire you to do actual investigative work. The very same work that got Devlin killed.

Mac examined the coffee table in front of the giant rear projection television. There was an empty box. The box had a picture of what looked like some sort of technology that one would purchase from the local Busy Bee electronics store. A store pick up slip stuck to the box partially blocking the full product picture. There was text right below the sticker. Mac strained his eyes. His brow furrowed.

"Upload footage with GoGo Cloud. Free up to 500 gigabytes," Mac said.

Devlin purchased a small GoGo camera. The kind athletes and outdoorsman used to take footage of their hikes, bike rides, extreme sports, hunting, etc. Vince could have missed it.

Mac pulled out his phone.

"Macky tacky. What's happening? No, wait. I don't care. Just write already! Gotta go!" Vince answered.

"Don't hang up! Devlin bought a GoGo camera. Did you find anything like that in or around the crashed car?"

"Yes, we did. It was destroyed. I even gave it to a good tech guy I know. He says it's wasted. Not much to do with it. I would have told you if it was something, Mac. Just write your book and let me do this."

"You are right. You are right. Fine." Mac sighed.

"Okay, next time you call, your ass is going straight to voicemail. Got it."

"What if it's an emergency?"

"Call nine-one-one." Vince ended the call.

Mac almost opened up the document for his manuscript. Ready to follow Vince's advice and just let

GPD figure the mess out. His food arrived. A big plate of eggs, bacon, and orange slices now supplemented with a smaller plate stacked with three pancakes. Mac's stomach grumbled.

Time to eat.

CHAPTER TWENTY

Millie couldn't wait to leave. Mr. Salem kept making comments about how great upstate New York was. Constantly bothering her about her decision. She politely declined to answer in four different ways at least seven different times.

The bank picked up for a while and she'd helped the tellers, but now it slowed back down. She did a quick Internet search on Perry Schroeder to see if she could jog her memory and lift the fog that Ditzy Dolores cast over her mind.

He was a contractor and built a lot of homes in the area. She didn't know why she didn't think to call her dad earlier. Hank Paderson worked for Schroeder for many years as a carpenter and siding extraordinaire.

Millie stood up and went upstairs to the empty

office space. Her phone in hand. Dad queued up on the contact list.

"Good morning, favorite daughter." Hank's voice always exuded an extra pep in the morning hours.

"Ha! Hey, Dad, how is it going?" Millie smiled. She did have a great dad.

"Going well. The Hawks are on later today and your mother is at yoga. So, things are great!"

"I am sure you are enjoying the peace and quiet. Hey, Dad, you worked with Perry Schroeder, right?"

"Yes, yes, I did. I did the siding for a lot of his homes, even helped with framing when he used to do that work himself too. He helped build our house, and I helped build his and his old partner's. Haven't seen or talked to him in years, though."

"Sorry to say, Dad, that he died last night. Mac and I were in the room." Millie paced the floor and walked over to a window and looked out at the gray, Midwestern sky.

"What? Wow! What happened? Where were you?"

"At the Potter House for a—like a murder mystery dinner experience. He may have shot himself, but we are currently investigating. What can you tell me about him?"

"Suicide? Perry? I mean, he was a demanding guy. Wanted to get things up quickly with quality.

'Quickly with Quality' was his mantra. He said it all the time on the job and to every customer he ever had." Hank's enthusiastic voice settled into a serious tone.

"He wasn't exactly the nicest guy."

"No, but nowhere near the meanest, just a serious guy. Serious about his work. He and Mitch eventually split. They didn't get along after a while."

"Who is Mitch?"

"Mitch Halliburton. He was a worker's boss. Listened to us and was okay with delaying things if the job called for it. More of a Union guy. Perry wanted results and quickly. Mitch broke off and created his own company. Halliburton construction. I did work for him too. Mitch was way more fun."

"Did they compete against each other for jobs?"

"All the time. It was rough. They had some epic rivalries, but what they didn't understand is that the market around here was big enough for both of them."

"Did it ever get ugly?"

"I mean, they did get upset with each other, but they never came to blows or anything like that. You have to remember they were best friends for a long time."

"But the job split them apart. They couldn't separate their personal and professional lives."

"You can say that. Yes."

"Okay, thanks, Dad. I really appreciate it. I should really get back to work here."

"No problem. If you need anything else, just let me know. If I remember anything specific about Perry that I think will help I will give you a call."

"Sounds good. Thanks, Dad."

"Yep. Bye." Hank ended the call or at least tried to. Millie heard him fumbling around with the phone. Millie pictured him putting on his glasses to figure out how to end the call. Even though he'd done it many, many times.

She mercifully ended the call. She dialed Mac's number.

"Millsies, what is happening?"

"Do you and your brother constantly change people's names?"

"It is probably an O'Malley family thing, so yes. Anyway, what is up?" Mac audibly slurped his coffee in Millie's ear.

"Are you—are you done slurping your coffee?" Millie rubbed her forehead.

"Ha! Sorry. How may I help you?"

"Just got done talking to my dad about Perry. He worked with him and his partner for years. Said that Perry was very serious most of the time and his partner wasn't and they split off from each other and went into competition with each other for construction contracts. Could be something to look into."

"Was the name of the partner Halliburton?" Mac asked.

"Yes, how did you know?"

"Edna Hern said she hired Halliburton after the hasty and sloppy construction of her house by none other than the Schroeder Construction company."

"Could be something to look into. Dad said Mitch and Perry were once best friends too. Who knows? Maybe the competition got downright nasty," Millie said.

"This is good stuff. I will let Vince know. Wouldn't hurt to see what Halliburton has to say. Great work, magical Millie!"

"No problem. I feel like we should have a nice dinner inside tonight and just relax." Millie walked down the stairs from the empty office.

"I agree. We can watch a movie or something too."

The beep of another call sounded in Millie's ear.

"Oh boy, it's my dad. I will call you back in a bit. See you later."

"Okay, say hi to Hank for me. Tell him I watched all the Bigfoot documentaries he suggested," Mac said.

"Oh Lord, I will. I will. Bye."

Millie ascended the stairs to the empty office again. "Dad."

"Interesting news. Just read in the paper that Mill Creek, a huge new golf course and residential development on the west end of Geneva, was just awarded to Schroeder Construction. I bet you Mitch and Perry fought hard for that job."

"Yeah, maybe even to the death. Wow. Thanks, Dad."

CHAPTER TWENTY-ONE

The pancakes went down smoothly. Smooth and savory from all the butter and syrup that Mac spread and poured over the carbohydrate packed breakfast food. Finish the pancakes and relay a possible lead to Vince provided by Millie and Hank. Mac had every intention of finishing his breakfast then working hard on his memoir. The home stretch of the story neared. His energy had renewed from the prospect of actually finishing his first draft. Tonight, he and Millie would enjoy a nice dinner and movie. The police work would be left to his brother. He felt good about it. Time to just let it go. Accept his retirement.

Pancakes did wonders for his disposition.

His phone buzzed on the table. Millie.

"That was fast. Don't you have work to do?"

"Dad just called and there was a write-up in the

Herald about a new construction on the west side of Geneva called Mill Creek."

"Yes, and?"

"I am not finished. The job was awarded to Schroeder Construction."

"Possible motive. Mitch Halliburton is upset that a multimillion-dollar construction goes to his chief rival and he offs him. That can work!" Mac felt the instincts kick back in. The desire to keep working on the case was innate. His journey to sated retirement came to another abrupt halt. He couldn't help himself. Once he started to feel okay about being out, something pulled him back in.

"Let me know what else you find out about it. I have to help close the bank soon. Love ya."

"Love you too." Mac ended the call and pulled back from his pancakes. He pushed them to the side and grabbed the MacBook once more to continue examining pictures.

Mac never closed the zoomed GoGo cam picture. He examined it once more.

"The GoGo cloud!" Mac yelled.

Juan looked at him and laughed.

"Sorry! Gotta make a call." Mac grabbed his phone and scrolled down his contact list to the Hanks household.

"Hello." Mikey Hanks answered the call.

"Mikey, it's Officer O'Malley. You wouldn't happen to know Devlin's GoGo Cam cloud account information, would you?"

"Oh yes, I helped him set it up. He went to Busy Bee to get a new phone and activate the data plan for the cam."

"Is it possible that he uploaded the footage?"

"I think once you set it up it just uploads to the cloud as soon as you stop the recording. It also does live recordings too. We set his account to private, of course, you know private investigator. Again, I didn't think he would actually start doing any real work until spring. Let me log in."

"Thank you. Maybe there is something on the account." Mac heard the audible clacking of Mikey's keyboard.

Audible breaths. A gasp. Heavier breathing sounded in Mac's ear.

"No, Devlin. Um, Officer O'Malley, you have to see this."

CHAPTER TWENTY-TWO

After Mikey had described what he saw in the GoGo Cam footage, Mac didn't waste any time. He went straight to Vince with the login information. Mac drove right into the parking lot, perhaps with a speed not befitting of the legal limit. He didn't care.

A uniformed policeman walking to his squad threw his hands up in the air. "Are you frickin' kidding me, man?"

Mac parked the car right in front of the glass doors and tall, blue window-paned front entrance of the Geneva police station. He hopped out without the use of his cane.

"Hey! What the hell do you think you are doing?" The uniform's footfalls sounded behind Mac.

"My brother is Detective Vince O'Malley and I need to get in there and talk to him about the

Schroeder death. I have a key lead that can help. I am sorry. I will move the car in a minute." Mac didn't even bother to turn around and entered the police station.

The front desk clerk stood up, slightly alarmed. "Can I help you, sir?"

"Vince in?"

"Oh yes, duh, you are Mac, the hero of the Chicago marathon! Nice to meet you!" The clerk picked up the phone and dialed Vince. "Your brother is here."

"Hey, he can't park there!" The uniform walked in.

"Relax, he is Vince's brother." The desk clerk smiled.

The uniform threw his hands up and walked out.

"Yeah, I am Vince's brother." Mac turned to the uniform.

"Mac, what the hell are you doing here? This better be good." Vince sipped his thermal mug. Probably his fifth tankard of caffeine today.

"THE FOOTAGE on this camera is for the private use of Hanks Investigations." Devlin mounted the camera on the front grill of his car. The screen had a digital time stamp of 5:33 p.m. on 2/14/20. The camera showed a wide angle of the Busy Bee parking lot then Randall Road. Devlin headed into Geneva.

His journey lasted a few minutes before he parked on a residential street near downtown.

The car didn't move for quite some time. Around 7:00 p.m. a black pickup truck drove into the frame. It pulled into a driveway about three houses down on the right side of the street. The passenger side of the truck showed. No one exited the vehicle from that side. No ID of the driver.

"Stop the footage. Back it up and freeze the plate." Mac put his hand on Vince's computer screen.

"Got it. Running the plate now."

"I bet you it's Halliburton."

"Mitchell Halliburton."

"How did you know that?" Vince looked up at his brother, who was hovering over his shoulder.

"Millie's dad worked with Schroeder and Halliburton on a lot of contracts. Apparently, there was no bigger clash of real estate titans than these two. They were former best friends and competed for every big contract in the area. Just recently, Halliburton lost a huge job to Schroeder. The new Mill Creek golf course and residential area." Mac talked fast with purpose.

"I would say that that would merit some hard feelings. Let's pay him a visit. Shall we? What else does this footage show?"

"At about 7:15 p.m., the truck stops at a bar on the

corner of Third Street and Route 38. But Devlin peels off before the driver exits the truck, possibly Mitch, and goes to eat at a drive thru then goes to the parking lot at the Riverside apartments and about an hour later the car spins and drives into the tree. The footage stops." Mac wanted to get to Mitch as soon as possible.

"Let me scrub through this for just a bit longer. We need to know how long the car was parked at Riverside and then match it up with the timeline of Perry's death. See if they match." Vince urged patience.

"Vince, they are close enough. Leave the technical stuff to someone here. We know that we have to talk to Halliburton and fast. Let's go." Mac put a hand on his brother's shoulder.

"Okay. Jackson, comb through this footage and let me know if you find anything of note. Let's head to Halliburton's house." Vince pointed to his partner. His official partner anyway. The one employed by the city of Geneva, not his brother.

CHAPTER TWENTY-THREE

The O'Malley brothers walked to the Halliburton house nestled on the end of Seventh Street in a cul-de-sac. The street matched the footage. The pickup truck's first stop. House may not be the proper description. More like mansion. A modern build with a sprawling wraparound porch and from the looks of the tall windows. Tall ceilings with a raised hallway behind a massive chandelier fit for royalty. The exterior brick was salmon-colored definitely washed or treated to get the proper look. Must have cost a fortune to do.

The black pickup truck was nowhere to be found.

Vince naturally reached the door first as he was not hindered by a debilitating and chronic leg injury like his brother. He knocked.

A large man with gray hair and white beard

answered with a charcoal gray activewear shirt on. He wasn't large from fat but built with muscle and testosterone treatments for men over forty.

"Good morning. I usually don't answer for solicitors, but I am in a good mood this morning. Whatever it is I won't take it but give me the spiel anyway," presumed Mitch said.

"We aren't solicitors. GPD would you like to ask you a few questions. Do you have a few minutes? Are you Mitch?" Vince flashed his badge.

"Whoa. Yes, Mitch Halliburton. Sure. What's going on, Officer?" Mitch put his huge stone-like hand out for Vince to shake.

"Perry Schroeder died last night at the Potter House. Gunshot wound to the head." Vince shook his hand.

Mac refused. Noted that Mitch didn't want them in the house. They all stood in the doorway.

"Perry was an old friend and colleague and one hell of a builder. This is awful. Someone shot him? Or did he off hims—"

"We will ask the questions," Mac chimed in.

"Fine. Go right ahead." Mitch shot a tense look at him.

"Firstly, where were you last night at around 7:30 p.m.?"

"I was at the LakeLawn resort in Wisconsin. I go

up there and icefish on Lake Delavan. Call the resort. They will concur. Now if you'll excuse me it is cold, and I don't have to answer any more of your questions." Mitch began to shut the door on the detective duo.

Mac put his cane on the door to stop the close. "Where is your black pickup truck?"

"My son, Mitchell, drives a black pickup truck. Have a good day, Officers." Halliburton pushed the door shut. Mac nearly lost his balance.

"Shit. Let's get out of here, Mac. Let's call Lake-Lawn and see if his alibi checks out. We still have details to look into." Vince grabbed Mac's forearm to help him regain his balance.

"He lied and said they were friends. They were not friends according to Millie's dad. Gosh, every time I think we have something. We run into a giant roadblock. In this case, he was a legitimately ginormous roadblock. He was jacked. Like Schwarzenegger in Conan built." Mac planted his cane in the porch planks and walked back to the car.

"He was huge. Still, why was Devlin Hanks spying on the Halliburton household? Something doesn't add up," Vince said.

"I mean, they are an affluent family and probably have their fair share of enemies. Who knows? Better call LakeLawn." Mac pulled out his phone as he opened the car door. He did a search for the number and called.

"They won't just offer up information like that from you without ID you're a cop," Vince said.

"I got this." Mac dialed LakeLawn resort.

"Mac just let me call." Vince started the car.

"Shush."

A pleasant female voice greeted Mac, "LakeLawn resort. Michelle here. What can I do for you?"

"Hello, hello, I was there last night. I seem to have left my phone in my room. Name is Mitch Halliburton." Mac used his best deep voice impression of Halliburton. Mac was a man of many talents.

"Oh, Mr. Halliburton, I am sorry to hear that. What was your room number?"

"I will be honest. I drank a bit too much out on the lake yesterday and I can't remember. I just know I made it back somehow. Haha!"

"I do see that you were here the past two nights. Now I remember you definitely weren't in the best shape last night. Haha! Thanks so much for being a frequent guest, Mr. Halliburton. I will personally look for it for you. Shall I call you back on this number?" Michelle's bubbly voice grated Mac's ear.

Mac slapped his forehead. No dice. "Yes, this number is just fine. Thanks, Michelle. Say what time did I stumble in last night?"

"I honestly don't remember an exact time, Mr. Halliburton. I'm sorry. I will get back to you soon about your phone."

"No worries. Thanks." Mac ended the call.

"That wasn't even a good impression of him." Vince shook his head.

"Did you smell the hangover on that guy? Thought it was worth a shot." Mac also shook his head.

"He did smell like booze and he was trying to sweat it out quick. You got lucky and I could have called anyway. That was unnecessary. You idiot."

"Yes, but my way was way more fun. LakeLawn is not that far away. He could have driven back and forth."

"Maybe, but we have a staff member who corroborated both a reservation and a physical ID of the guy. We gotta keep working. I am running out of steam, though." Vince shared.

"You just keep going. I am done. I gotta get off the rollercoaster and finish my book already. I am not a cop anymore."

"Before you hang it up for good this time, which we both know isn't happening, you need to call Hank real quick. See if Mitch has a son named Mitch." Vince looked at his brother. They neared the blue and white police station.

"I don't have my girlfriend's dad's phone number. Why would I have that?"

"Call Millie then."

"Okay, I will, just drop me off by my car near the door. I will call her and get back to you. Please spare me any details Jackson may have found. You just handle it from here, please." Mac opened the door that aligned directly with his car door in front of the station. Frustrated and out of patience, Mac O'Malley realized he didn't have to worry about solving any more murders. He really didn't. Right?

CHAPTER TWENTY-FOUR

Millie completed a few more transaction entries as the afternoon approached. Closing time. Mr. Salem did stop hovering and left a few minutes ago. The smile on her face and the promise of a relaxing evening displayed her relief. She'd thought that she'd figured out her answer about the job promotion. Still, she needed a bit more time to sort things through. She knew how she felt about her life here and especially, life with Mac. She felt a permanence to their relationship. A confidence she'd never felt before.

Her phone buzzed on her desk. Speak of the devil. "Hello, Mac. Almost done with work. Any updates?"

"Honestly, the update is we are running into issues and blocks and barriers and really have no evidence other than weapons, etc. I am going to let Vince handle it from here. Does Mitch Halliburton have a son named Mitch?"

"I don't know off hand. No worries. I can ask Dad. Let me call you right back. You at the Wanderer? Want me to meet you there?" Millie logged out of her computer.

"Yes, that works. See you in a few. Love ya." Mac sounded defeated.

"Love you too. It will be a better rest of the day. Bye." Millie ended the call. She pulled back from her desk and contemplated a risky move. Not physically risky but perhaps relationship risky. Would Mac freak out and run away? Millie knew he probably would not do that. I mean, how could he do better than her?

He couldn't.

She laughed to herself then made the call to her sister, Angela.

"Hello." Angela's voice sounded irritated as if Millie dare to call her.

"Hey, how are you?" Millie stood up and walked to the coat rack.

"Paige and Johnny are driving me insane. They won't stop irritating each other. Don't have kids," Millie's sister warned.

"I will keep that in mind. Hey, was wondering if you could do me a quick favor?"

"Will you take your niece and nephew to live at your place permanently? Then it's a definite yes."

Millie laughed. "Well, not so sure about that. Seriously, though, could you do a couple sketches for me?"

"Sketches? Of what?"

"Memory sketches."

"Millie, I don't have the ingredients for that today and I can't make it to Sycamore for more. Johnny, put that down! Now."

"If I get the ingredients could you do it, today? Mac and I are helping Vince with a possible murder and need to recreate the scene because we are completely stuck. Maybe the sketch will reveal something we hadn't seen before. It's for a good cause."

"Fine. I will do it. Come over later. Let me clean up in here first. Do not hit each other with those! I gotta go. It's fine. See you later. I am not kidding about you taking the kids, though."

"Haha thanks. See you later."

"Bye."

Memory sketches could help fill in the blanks. Possibly even illuminate the moment the shot was fired into Perry's head. Magic may help Mac and Millie crack yet another case.

CHAPTER TWENTY-FIVE

Mille's mother, Becca, after fiddling with her blond hair for a considerable chunk of the past hour, gave up and just decided to put it up in ponytail.

"Hank! Are you ready?"

"Bec, I have been waiting for the past hour. We are just picking up lumber not going to a nice restaurant!"

"Hank. Stop yelling. I have a headache." Becca walked down the stairs in her home at 272 WitchHazel Circle.

"Can we go now?" Hank put his hands up in frustration.

Becca's phone rang from somewhere in the house.

"Hank, where's my phone?"

"I have no idea. Sounds like the kitchen."

"Big help. Idiot." Becca walked past him in the front hall and turned back toward the kitchen.

Her phone lay on the counter next to her purse. "Hello."

"Hey, Mom, do you have any ingredients for memory magic?" Millie asked.

"Oh no. I don't right now. Why? What do you need memory magic for?" Becca fished her purse for some of her doctor-prescribed migraine pills. Even she wanted to avoid Ditzy Dolores.

"Mac and I need it for the case we are working on."

"Oh, your dad told me about Perry Schroeder. That is terrible. Is this a thing now? You and Mac helping the police solve murders sounds like a TV series or something. Am I right?" Becca asked.

"We just happened to be in the room when Perry died. It does sort of feel like it is becoming a thing. Anyway, do you have anything to help? I could grab whatever we need anyway. Just wondering what exactly I do need as well."

"Millie, don't even worry about it. Hank and I are heading to Sycamore to get some more reclaimed wood for that table we are building and I can pick up the ingredients then. Did you want to come over later for dinner and get them?"

"Actually, if you could head to Angela's that would be great. She is going to do a memory sketch for us," Millie said.

"Perfect. We will grab what you need then head to your sister's."

"Oh wait, Mom, could you ask Dad if Mitch Halliburton had a son named Mitch?"

"I think he did. Do you really trust your father to know? I am kidding. Hank, Millie needs to know if Mitch has a son named Mitch?"

"Yes, he does. Mitch Junior!" Hank said.

"Hank. Why are you still yelling? I am right in front of you. Anyway, I assume you heard that." Becca glared at Hank.

"Yes, thank you. Mitch Junior. I will see you later at Angela's. I think like four-ish works. Thanks, Mom."

"No problem, buh bye."

"Bye." Millie ended the call.

"We have to stop at the Morris shop after we get the wood." Becca swallowed her headache pill without any water.

"Why? That place gives me the creeps like you give me the creeps." Hank laughed.

"I hope it does with the way you have been acting today." Becca did crack a smile at her husband's attempt at levity.

CHAPTER TWENTY-SIX

The Morris Shop was actually hidden inside the Morris Garden and Greenhouse. A place to buy plants, seeds, Christmas trees, saplings, etc. If one walked into the old red brick building next to the greenhouse, the shop was actually all the way in the back in the corner. If one wanted to enter said shop in the back corner of said red brick building, you had to give the magic word, which was Gaia. Gaia, which in Greek mythology was not even considered a god or goddess but a female titan, a primordial deity. One of the original deities to make up the cosmos just as important as the titan father of Zeus, Kronos. Kronos represented time and Gaia represented nature or the earth.

It was this fact that unsettled Hank, for nature in

the magical world meant nature in all its beauty and degradation.

"Gaia," Becca said the magic word.

Around them as if the shop were being built and recorded with a time-lapse camera the shop appeared in the back corner. Vines grew and overtook the red brick. A long row of jars, containers, various animal skulls and bones, along with the most beautiful, rare plants on the earth populated the counter with colors so vibrant that Hank always tried to focus on the plant life and not the dead animals floating in the jars and various body parts from creatures from all corners of the planet. The shop could be confused for just a really long counter as it was in one with a small space behind the counter for the clerk to mill about and help.

It defied logic that an extremely long counter could exist in the corner of the red-brick building, but it did. Again, if one spoke the magic word, a small part of the magic world appeared. Unfortunately, magic words were needed to remain hidden. Witch trials did happen throughout history and well, it was just better this way.

"Becca and Hank, what brings you in today?" Marie, the clerk of the Morris Shop, stood in all black with the typical black and pointed witch hat.

"Very traditional outfit today, Marie. You look good in black," Becca commented.

"Thank you very much. Hank, always good to see you. You okay?" Marie asked.

"I am fine." Hank stayed near the end of the counter closest to the exit as his wife perused the shop.

"We are here for fish wax melts and burners. Preferably the DHC enriched kind not the boney kind."

"The type you want really smell bad, Becca. I ran out of the lavender-enhanced ones. Are you sure?" Marie asked.

"Yes, we need them. It will be fine. The kids will get over it." Becca reached into her purse for some currency.

"Suit yourself." Marie snapped her fingers. A small cigar box appeared on a small space between a jar of frog legs and another jar of locust shells. Marie pinched her nose.

"I just need two melts and the burners, I suppose."

"You can have the whole box in fact, for free. Just get it out of here." Marie even with a pinched nose waved her free hand.

"Great. Thanks. I think I have burners at home actually. Hank, this will be good for us. We can have the ones the kids don't use. Keeps the brain sharp and the memory strong." Becca reached into the narrow space between the jars and picked up the cigar box of smelly fish wax melts.

"Bec, how are you not sick to your stomach?" Hank covered his nose and mouth with both hands.

"Oh, grow up. It isn't that bad." Becca committed to the whole box.

"You can't be serious. You are going to bring that in the car? Can't you do a smell spell?" Hank asked.

"I admit. It is pretty bad. Still, anything for the kids, Hank."

"Are they really all that great? Let's be honest."

Becca laughed out loud then quickly covered her nose and mouth.

CHAPTER TWENTY-SEVEN

Millie and Mac enjoyed a relatively quiet afternoon. They ate some lunch at the Tiny Wanderer and talked about the case a little, but that didn't dominate the conversation. Millie wanted to talk about the promotion, but it wasn't the right time. She did say that she needed to stop at Angela's. Millie looked at the clock in her car, which read 3:45 p.m. Mac sat in the passenger seat along for the ride.

"Ready for this?" Millie pulled her car into a secluded driveway in St. Charles, Illinois.

"Sure. I haven't met your sister yet. It will be fun."

"She isn't exactly the warmest person to be around. She also doesn't do hugs or anything, so don't give your goodbye hug. Or maybe you should try so you can see her face."

"Ha! I am so going to try. Her husband's name is Jacob?"

"Yes, but I think he is ice fishing this weekend."

"That is a popular thing to do around here."

Millie and Mac exited Millie's black sedan and walked to the front door of a charming ranch-style home replete with gray siding and white shutters around every window. A very rustic chic look. Millie let her and Mac in. The interior kept the same look with some warmer reclaimed wood tones and wood flooring with some gray and copper décor on the fireplace and walls with many frames with pics of the family.

Millie liked her sister's house. Her sister she loved but didn't always like. Their relationship wasn't exactly close nor was it bad. It just sort of existed. Millie and Angela were two very different people.

"Hey. You must be Mac. I am Angela." Angela greeted them from the kitchen area, a hard right from the front door.

"Hello, Angela, nice to finally meet you! Really love your house. It's very nice." Mac smiled.

"Hey, thanks for doing this. I am sure it won't take long. Where are the kids?"

"Jacob's parents took them out for dinner. Good riddance. Mac, you want a beer or anything?" Angela loosened up if only a little.

"No, no, thanks. I am good. Maybe in a bit. What is Angela doing exactly?" Mac looked at Millie while removing his jacket.

"I will let you handle this." Angela looked at Millie then walked into the kitchen.

"We are here to see if we can recreate the moment Perry died with..."

"With what, Millie?" Mac looked curious.

"Magic and Angela's talents as an artist. Please don't freak out."

"Millie, why would I freak out? I think this whole magic thing is amazing. I try not to ask too many questions about it because you tell me not to and that you will let me know more about it in due time. Today is one of those times! Let's do it! What do we do? Time travel or something? And now you are saying your sister is magical too? Are you all magical? Is it only you two or are there more?" Mac let out a lot of supressed excitement for Millie's mad magic skills.

"Helloooo!" Becca walked in the front door followed by Hank.

"Hey, Mom. Hey, Dad," Millie greeted her parents. Angela didn't emerge from the kitchen.

"You guys, I am just warning you that we left the wax melts in the trunk. They smell pretty bad. I thought we should set the burners up first." Becca walked in.

Hank looked tired and like he didn't want to be there.

"I can burn some sage to offset the smell." Angela met them in the front hall.

"Wait. Your mom is magical too?" Mac's jaw dropped.

MILLIE DIDN'T HAVE to worry about Mac's comfort level. He let Becca wrap the blindfold around his head with no objection.

Millie reached to her right to find his hand and hold it. Her blindfold was tied tight and threatened to increase the pain of her usual headache, but the pain level held steady at a solid five out of ten. She'd found Mac's hand. "Okay, now we have to activate our memories to the moment before Perry passed. The waiter was bringing bread over. Do you remember that, Mac?"

"Yes. How could I forget? It just happened last night."

"Are you sure? We all know you can be a bit dumb-ish," Becca commented from behind them.

Mac and Millie laughed.

"I am ready," Mac said.

"Mom, put the melts on the burners," Millie ordered.

Millie, moments before, placed two wax melt burners in front of Mac and herself. She placed them there so the vapors from the melts would enter their nostrils directly, ensuring the effectiveness of brain-activating properties.

"Angela, you ready?" Millie asked.

"Yes. The wax melts smell absolutely disgusting. Let's get this over with. Don't even thing about puking on my table. Memoriam Experian Translatio," Angela spoke, presumably over the wax melts.

"Hang in there, you two," Hank's voice said.

Millie heard Angela drop the melts on the burners. The fish wax melts did smell absolutely like rotted fish.

"Mac, I know it smells bad but focus on your memories from the bread service forward. We don't want to have to do this again." Millie squeezed his hand.

"Oh, dear Lord. I feel like I licked all the fish on display in the seafood section! Ack." Mac struggled.

"Can you manage to take a couple deep breaths? Let's do it and then we will be done and try to run through your memory from the bread service to you walking over and examining the body too."

"Keep it going, you guys. Almost there," Angela said.

Millie heard the audible scratching of pencil on

paper. Some broad strokes, some short, some slower. Her sister sketched out their memories onto paper.

"Blah!" Mac yelped.

"Almost there. Please don't puke on my table. I am going to need you to both give me one more deep breath. We almost got this."

"I can't! I hate fish! Why fish?" Mac yelled.

"Yes, you can, Mac. It's okay. Let's do it together. Deep breath!" Millie comforted and rubbed his hand.

"Blah! Okay, I got one more in me!" Mac sucked in more vapors. Millie followed then heard more intense sketching from her sister across the table. A masterful maneuvering of pencil to paper. She was excited to see their memories. Millie removed her blindfold.

"Okay. Okay, good. Take off the blindfolds and, Mom, open the windows. Open everything and get those things out of here." Angela stood up from the table, rubbing her forearm and wrist.

Hank and Becca both grabbed the rancid burners and put them in the backyard through the patio door next to the dining room. Mac followed them outside to get fresh air.

Millie looked across the table at the poster paper adorned with rough sketches of the cursed Valentine Dine or Die event.

CHAPTER TWENTY-EIGHT

Millie looked over the drawings. Angela did a great job in a very short amount of time. Her sister was many things. Talented artist being one of the redeeming qualities.

"I think I need to bathe in air fresheners." Mac walked back in the house with his forearm across his mouth.

"Take a look at this. We need to see if all this trouble was worth it." Millie pointed to the poster paper adorned with a series of storyboards. Square pictures that recreated the time period right before to right after Perry's death.

"It's split into two sections. I can add some shading if you want. Make it clearer. It is still pretty rough," Angela said.

"No, I think this will work. How did you do this so fast? Wait. I know. Magic," Mac said.

"Well, yes. I made it go faster with an enchanted spell on the pencil as well to get that damn smell out of my house. My hand is still a little sore."

"Oh, of course." Mac laughed.

Millie examined the poster. She pored over the pic then pointed. "The top is your perspective, Mac."

"It would appear so."

The top sequence showed Mac noticing the server bringing bread. In the background, Rachel and Perry sat in front of each other. Perry sat in front of the radiator coils and the open window. Then the images were muddied, less clear as to what was going on.

"That series of pics must have been when the lights went out. Still there are some details our brain fills in even with the lights out." Millie pointed to some outlines of people and even with the lights out the brain could still map out the space of the room. One outline stood out in the foreground. When the light turned off, Mac looked across the table at Millie. On the left side of the sketch was a small light. Possibly a muzzle flash?

"Look at your pics, Millie. Maybe we can spot a difference. Something I didn't see." Mac stood next to Millie as their eyes strained at every detail.

Millie didn't look at Mac when the lights turned

back on. The clarity of the sketches returned. Millie looked toward the sound of the .38 firing. Perry now slumped in his chair. His chin rested on his chest. Rachel had placed her hands on each side of her face and started to scream again.

"Do you see anything different?" Mac shook his head.

At this point both the top sketches and bottom sketches looked at Rachel and Perry, except Mac's perspective moved closer to them. Perry's body fell over. The radiator coils were now exposed.

"That's it!" Millie scanned the whole poster then slowed her gaze on some key details in the background. Double-check.

"What? I don't see anything different." Mac's eyes panned the last few sketches of him examining Perry's body.

"How did we miss this?" Millie pumped a fist in the air.

"Millie. What?" Mac asked then looked at her family now huddled around the table with them.

Hank, Becca, and Angela said in unison, "What, Millie?"

"The window was open when the lights were on and when the lights went back on the window was closed!"

"Who was close enough to shut the window? Who was around the window? Anyone?"

The whole family and Mac looked at the pictures. The only two people close enough to the window were Rachel and Perry. The other couples were in their seats and the server was close to Mac and Millie.

"Perry didn't kill himself. He was shot by someone on the porch. The killer then handed the gun to Rachel, who nervously and sloppily placed the gun in Perry's right hand. I knew it looked strangely positioned in his hand." Mac now paced the living room.

"Rachel quickly shut the window and screamed to block the sound of her closing the window. She went back to her seat and the lights went back on. Then screamed again for dramatic effect," Millie added.

"She also didn't have her gloves on after she left the bathroom. She must have known that residue would have been on them. Could you do the magic memory thing again for the bathroom conversation you had with Rachel?" Mac asked.

"No, that won't work. I don't have any recollection whatsoever because of taking Ditzy Dolores. Doesn't matter anyway. We know we have to bring in Rachel for more questioning. She helped murder her own husband. But why? Dad, what do you know about Perry's wife Rachel?" Millie looked at Hank.

"I don't know much. I just know that she was around when Perry and Mitch broke up their business and went into competition with each other," Hank said.

"So, she did know Mitch. Probably was even close friends with him." Mac rubbed his chin.

"We need to pay a visit to Rachel Waddle. If she isn't in Cabo or something for the weekend." Millie's eyes were wide with excitement.

"Wait a minute! How did she know the lights were going to go off at that exact moment? Seems a bit fantastic to me," Hank asked.

"Rutherford said the lights were supposed to go out at that time. He could have informed them beforehand. We can talk to him and see if Rachel or Perry asked about it for whatever reason," Mac said.

"Wait. Check your ticket. Does it give a warning of effects and darkness? It probably does." Millie pointed to Mac.

Mac grabbed his wallet and pulled out the fresh stub. "It does mention the lights going out but doesn't give an exact time. We should call the number on this ticket and ask Rutherford. In the meantime, let's get to Rachel's house now."

CHAPTER TWENTY-NINE

"You sure we shouldn't call Vince?" Millie and Mac parked in front of the house her father said was the Schroeder home in Wayne, Illinois, a small and extremely opulent town north of St. Charles and Geneva.

"What do we tell Vince? We used magic to recreate the night Perry was killed. He will laugh in our faces. We have to get in there and find the gloves she wore or force a confession. That reminds me I should call Rutherford. What a name. Do you think that is just a stage name? Can't be his real name." Mac fumbled for the ticket stub.

"Mac, just call him already."

"On it."

"Hello. Dine or Die Productions."

"Is Rutherford there, please?"

"Haha yes, I am Danny. I play Rutherford."

"Hey, Danny, Officer O'Malley. Just have a quick question. Did anyone request a script of the night's event beforehand?"

"Hey, you know Billy's mom Edith. She thinks you are a great guy. Billy plays one of our servers."

"Ah yes, thank you! That is nice."

Millie threw her hands up, urging Mac to get some answers.

"Sorry, Danny. I have to get going. Did anyone request information on the show's script or anything?"

"Yes, and it caused a big argument with my company. Rachel Waddle's security guard requested information. Claimed it was just for his client's safety and security. His name was Burke. We looked him up to see if he was legit and he is. Burke Protective Services."

"Ah, okay. Okay, thank you very much. That makes sense. A high-profile audience member may have security people. Makes sense. Thanks, Danny." Mac ended the call.

"Rachel did have advance knowledge of the show's theatrics!" Millie said.

"Yes, Burke is the name of the security guard. That is probably him right now. Let me handle him." Mac looked at another large beefy man akin to Mitch walk out to circle the driveway of Rachel's Wayne mansion. He looked right at Mac and Millie.

"Mac, let me handle him."

"What are you going to do? Put a spell on him?"

"With my looks naturally."

"Ha! Wait. Really?"

"No, you idiot. I will put an actual spell on him. He won't be a problem." Millie exited the car and walked the circle driveway of the Spanish mission-style home. It looked like Perry just copied the pirates attraction from the most popular theme park for his home. Mac really liked it. He realized he should stop gawking at the house and assist Millie. She was far ahead.

Big Burke put his hand up as if telling her to stop.

He heard Millie say something but couldn't quite figure it out.

Burke then fell to the ground in a heap right outside the front door.

"Oh, dear Lord, what happened?" Mac limped over as fast as he could. His cane in a vice grip.

"I just made him lose consciousness for a while. Not sure how long. We better get in there and question Rachel." Millie pointed her wand at the door.

"Whoa, whoa, easy, Ms. Earp! We can't just wand-sling our way through this. Why don't we just knock on the door first?" Mac put his hands up as if to tame Millie's aggression.

"Fine." Millie placed her wand in some sort of interior pocket of her winter jacket.

Mac walked to the large double wooden doors with large iron cast handles. He knocked.

No answer.

Again.

Nothing.

"Let me just unlock it. It's freezing out here." Millie reached for her wand.

The door swung open. America's morning ray of sunshine, Rachel Waddle, stood at the door. "Hello. Officer O'Malley, right?"

"Can we come in for a few minutes? Just have some quick questions about Perry." Mac and Millie both smacked up against each other's hips to block Rachel's view of the downed behemoth named Burke.

"Sure."

CHAPTER THIRTY

Rachel Waddle looked less like a ray of sunshine and more like a torrential downpour. Her mascara had run down on her face. Distraught and partially relieved after she'd shut the door behind Mac and Millie.

"What exactly are you two doing here? Didn't I answer all of the actual police's questions?" Rachel asked. Her demeanor shifted from just a few short seconds ago. Noted.

"Actually yes, Rachel. We know what you did. We have footage of you receiving the gun from whoever was outside the window and on the porch of the Potter House. You then placed the gun in Perry's freshly dead hand. You screamed and shut the window. Who was outside the window, Rachel? Who pulled the trigger, Rachel?" Mac's voice intensified the longer he spoke.

"Impossible. The lights were out. I had no idea what was going on." Rachel stood defiant.

"Rachel. Stop this. A confession will make this all go much smoother for you." Mac insisted. She was full of shit.

She rubbed the bridge of her nose. The rest of her face. Swollen with Botox.

"It was the perfect time to stage a suicide at the murder dinner show. Burke knew the exact moment the lights were to go out. He waited outside for the right moment. Then boom!" Mac pressed.

"No. Stop! I control the narrative. On Monday, America will know the tragedy of Perry's suicide. I did not do this! Get out!"

"Did Burke break in and turn up the heat so the staff would open a window? Did you open it before everyone arrived?" Mac pressed.

"Shut up!" Rachel began to shake.

"You killed Perry, Rachel. Your own husband. For what? What did Perry have on you? What did his Private Investigator catch you doing?"

Rachel walked to the stairs and grabbed the banister.

"Stop! Please! Stop!"

"Making your husband's death a suicide on Valentine's Day sure will bring out the pity parade for you and drive up the ratings, huh, Rachel?"

"He did this!" Rachel started crying then fell to the stairs.

"Who did what, Ms. Waddle?"

"His obsession with Mitch. He did this..." Rachel's voice faded into the carpet on the stairs.

"Who? Rachel. Who?" Mac moved closer to her.

"Perry! Perry did this! He hired a PI to spy on Mitch Halliburton and his meetings for the Mill Creek contract and that idiot PI caught Mitch and me..."

"You and Mitch what? What were you two doing?"

"Mitch and I were having an affair. Perry used the pictures and video that amateur idiot from the ballpark recorded to get Mitch to back down from the Mill Creek contract and threatened to leak the affair to the media and would have ruined my career. Perry made me feel like a prisoner. Made me stay with him. To control me. He was a sick man! Sick! He deserved to die!"

"Who pulled the trigger, Rachel? Was it Burke?"

"Mitch. Mitch did, not Burke. Leave that big oaf alone." Rachel cried with her head on the third step.

"Millie, make sure she doesn't go anywhere."

Mac walked outside and called Vince.

"Hello, bro."

"Get a couple squads over to the Schroeder mansion in Wayne. And get as many guys as you can to the Halliburton household now. Rachel just broke

94

JB MICHAELS

down. She and Mitch killed Perry and probably Devlin as well. I will explain more later. Just do it."

"If you say so, Mac. I will get dispatch to get every available squad on this."

Mac walked back in.

"I thought it was odd she chose the stairs to sprawl out and cry on. She faked her crying to do this." Millie held up Rachel's phone. The screen read, "They know. They are coming. Get away."

"Oh shit. She warned Mitch. We have to go now."

CHAPTER THIRTY-ONE

"Dormitabis Minimo." Millie pointed her wand at Rachel, who ran to the top of the stairs. She collapsed on the top floor.

"Oh my gosh! What if she would have fallen backward, Millie?" Mac put his hands on his head.

"She didn't. All is well. She will be out like Burke until the cops arrive here. We have to get to Mitch's house quickly. Driving won't be fast enough." Millie walked deeper into the mansion, searching for something.

"What are you doing? The car is this way!" Mac heard doors open and slam shut.

"Oh, good, good. You ready for this, Mac?" Millie stood with a broom in hand.

"What are you doing with a broo—oh you have got

to be kidding me." Mac put the cane into the plush area rug of the front hall and turned around.

"Mac, just grab a hold of me. It will be fine. Trust me. Mitch is probably getting away."

"Won't you be exposed? Isn't this too high-profile for witchdom?" Mac asked.

"Stop arguing. Let's go!" Millie ran past him and out of the house.

Mac tucked his cane under his arm and walked out behind her. Broom flight was the fastest option.

"This will get chilly and it's nighttime. No one will see us. Hang on tight."

Mac's heart beat hard and fast. His nerves were slightly calmed by hugging Millie. The broom moved between his legs. Millie jumped from the ground. The air of the cold winter's night bit Mac's ears and the rest of his face. He buried his face into Millie's back and closed his eyes.

"Oh, dear Looooord!" Mac yelled. He felt Millie gain speed. The wind's howl battered his ears. He still kept his eyes shut.

"Mac, just open your eyes. It's beautiful." Millie urged.

Mac reluctantly opened his eyes and looked down. The darkness of the Fox River Millie followed south toward Geneva lay directly below but was bordered by the yellow, ambient glow of the homes on the river-banks. He felt like Peter Pan flying over the Thames. They approached downtown St. Charles and could see the bridge and all the lights from the Hotel Baker, restaurants, and historic theater venues like the Arcada. It truly was a sight to see from so high up.

Mac calmed and felt more comfortable with each passing second. He shared a broom with his magical girlfriend Millie on the ride of his life. The next big cluster of lights was Geneva and the Rt. 38 bridge lay ahead.

"Make sure to take a right at the bridge and head southwest to the end of Seventh Street. Mitch's house is in a cul-de-sac there." Mac informed Millie.

"Got it. Hang on tight. We are going to dive in a minute or so." Millie's voice sounded happy, excited, and ready to get the bad guy.

Third Street's yellow lamp lights and brick crossing lanes repeated below. Mac smiled upon seeing the Tiny Wanderer below and the yellow awning of his favorite entrance. Millie turned and the couple was now over the darkness of the dimly lit neighborhood near downtown Geneva. Millie began her dive to Seventh Street.

Mac's stomach leapt into his throat and he wrapped his arms even tighter around Millie's waist. His cane he left wrapped around his wrist. And it dangled off the side and occasionally bumped his leg.

The street's icy and patchy pavement zoomed closer with each second of Millie's steep broom dive.

Mac felt his stomach retreat from his throat as Millie leveled the broom and gently landed them on Seventh Street. There were no signs of any squads nearby quite yet.

"What a ride." Mac let Millie pull the broom from between his legs.

"Incredible, isn't it? Being magical has its perks." Mille tossed the broom to the side.

"Looks like no one is here yet. His house has like pink brick and is down that way on the right side of the street. The one with the black pickup truck or should I say two black pickup trucks? There is another truck!" Mac fished his pockets for his phone to call Vince.

"Mac O'Malley?" a voice sounded from behind him and Millie.

"Yes?" Mac turned on the sidewalk.

"I am Officer Bermudez from GPD. Vince had me watch the house. No one has left all day. So, they are in there or on vacation or something. I was waiting for the rest of the GPD to get here before I went in." The plain-clothes policeman flashed his badge.

"No need to wait. We better just get in there. His girlfriend warned him we were coming. You sure no one has left? You check for a back door?"

"Yes, I have been out of the car roaming around the

house for a while. Again, he is either inside or on vacation."

"When did Vince assign you to this?"

"Earlier today like mid-afternoon."

"That was probably right after we talked to him. I guess there could be a small window of time he could have skipped town or left the house. Let's go see," Mac said.

Millie started walking to the house ahead of them.

Mac and Officer Bermudez followed.

"Enough talk, more action, I suppose." Mac shook his head.

The salmon-colored brick was accentuated by bloom lamps in the landscaping next to the house. The chandelier's light from the front hall cast a warm glow on the snowy grass and salted front path. Mille set foot on the wraparound porch first and knocked on the door.

No answer.

She knocked again.

"Geneva Police! Open up!" Millie yelled.

Mac and Bermudez looked at each other and laughed to ease the tension.

"Sorry, just always wanted to say that," Millie said.

Mac knocked one more time.

Nothing.

"From Rachel's confession, we certainly have probable cause to enter. Mitch is one giant dude, but with Mill—oh look!" Mac stopped himself from outing Millie's magical prowess and pointed in the direction from whence they came.

Millie shot a wide-eyed look at Mac and mouthed silently, "You idiot!"

Mac covered his mouth.

"Here comes the backup." Officer Bermudez observed four squad cars turning into the cul-de-sac.

CHAPTER THIRTY-TWO

Vince emerged from the passenger side of a squad car parked at the end of the driveway and ran to them.

"Hey, Vince. You pick up Rachel yet?" Mac asked.

"Yes, Wayne authorities picked her up a couple minutes ago. It was like she was on something. What's going on here?"

"The Halliburton fam is not answering the door." Millie knocked again.

"Doesn't matter. Let's get inside and search the house for him." Vince pulled out his gun from his holster.

"Yes, let us handle it from here," Bermudez said.

"No, no way. We are going in. We helped you get Gordon. We are helping you get Mitchy Halliburton." Mac insisted.

"Okay, fine. Just you, Mac. Bermudez, you and

me will clear the upstairs. Mac, get Jackson to go with you and take the ground floor. Oh, and be careful, another solid lead. The bullet that Devlin was shot with came from a hunter's rifle and sure enough Mitch has a hunting license and has registered a rifle that matches the bullet wound. It's a common hunting rifle but still. Be careful. Mac, you need a gun. Millie, stay out here. Mac was a cop. You are a banker." Vince had pulled out his gun-metal and brown handled .38 from his leg holster and handed it to his brother.

"How ironic. A .38. Mitch is a mountain of muscle and you give me this tiny gun."

"Oh stop. You wanted to go in. You need something to protect yourself." Vince shook his head.

Millie opened the door and let herself in.

"The door was open this whole time?" Vince asked.

"No idea. Don't ask. Millie, wait for us! Vince is right, you should stay out." Mac followed her into the front hall underneath the brightly lit grand chandelier.

"I am not leaving, so shut it all of you. Mac and I will search down here."

Vince opened his mouth to voice his protest.

"No. I am not leaving, Vince. Get upstairs." Millie already began her search for Mitch in the sitting room to the left of the front hall. Vince and Bermudez followed but took the stairs to the right. Up they went. Mac and Millie were presumably alone.

"Let's stick together," Mac said to Millie.

The house felt cold inside. Big and empty too. Maybe somehow Mitch escaped. Two pickup trucks and two people named Mitch Halliburton made the possibility that Mitch the older murderer could have driven to LakeLawn earlier and returned to kill Perry then drove back for the night to solidify his alibi. It wasn't that far of a drive. Devlin could have driven away from the pickup truck that stopped at the bar because he may have identified that it was Mitch Junior and not Mitch Senior. The man Devlin was tasked to keep tabs on by Perry Schroeder. Maybe Devlin didn't know they had similar pickup trucks.

Mac realized that those details would be sorted out soon enough and that now the hunt for the hunter and killer had commenced. Mac gripped the handle of his gun with probably too much force. He needed to relax, but it had been a long time since he'd cleared the interior of a building and the last time he did, he found a bomb that was set to blow out the front of a building and rain terror on Chicago marathon runners.

Mac's heart pounded. Sweat beaded on his forehead. He wiped it with his jacket. He looked up and realized he'd lost Millie.

"Mac, snap out of it. You have been standing here

for a while. I thought you were right behind me. I cleared the kitchen and the living room." Her voice burst into his ears from behind him.

"I am sorry. Sorry. Spaced out." Mac turned around.

"You okay?"

"Yes, yes, I am fine. What about the garage? We will check there next."

"Upstairs is clear! Even the damn attic. We will head to the basement," Vince yelled.

"So far no luck down here," Mac said.

Millie walked to the right side of the stairs and back to the kitchen. Mac followed.

The kitchen was vast with a large island in the middle of it with a granite top and white cabinetry all around. Mac and Millie walked to the far end of the kitchen and turned right. A powder room was to the right and the garage entry was on the wall in front of them. Just a regular door.

Millie let Mac reach the door first and stood behind him. He grasped the doorknob and peeked behind the door. The lights were out.

"Lights are not on and I don't have a flashlight. He could be anywhere in there."

Millie grabbed her wand from her jacket. "Open it slightly and I will send some light inside."

"Sounds good." Mac opened the door enough so that Millie's wand could fit through.

"Fireflies," Millie said as she put her wand into the garage. Her arm shook slightly with the force of her spell.

"Opening now." Mac pushed the door open. There was more than enough light in the garage as yellow and gold fireflies dotted the ceiling and flew all around in a majestic, dazzling light show.

"Mac. Focus." Millie entered the garage. It was empty of cars, but the side shelving had hunting and fishing gear on it.

"Looks like an outdoorsman store in here." Mac found the light switch and flipped it on. Millie's fireflies dissipated with the light.

"No luck. Where is this guy?" Millie secured her wand to her jacket pocket once more.

"Nothing in the basement either," Bermudez and Vince both said as they joined Mac and Millie in the garage.

"Something is not right. There must be someplace we haven't checked," Millie said. She pulled out her phone.

"Face it. He is not here," Vince said, defeated.

CHAPTER THIRTY-THREE

Millie tried to think of different spells and magic to use to find Mitch. Reditus Retorno, the one she'd used to track down Patricia's murderer, worked better outside of people's own homes. Magic could be finicky. A return-to-owner spell like Reditus Retorno used on Mitch would be ineffective and confused inside a place where everything was technically owned by Mitch and had Mitch's aura.

Unless.

"Open the garage door, Mac. I have to call my dad and I'm not getting a signal in here."

Mac hit a button next to the house entry and the large white garage door lifted to a view of two black pickups parked in the driveway.

Millie looked to the shelf and found a lure and

pocketed it quickly while the boys stood in a circle discussing what to do next.

She pulled out her phone and casually walked out onto the driveway then across the street away from Mitch's property. She looked at her phone as if trying to procure a better signal. Her phone was fine. With her other hand, she held the lure. She put the phone up to her ear and said, "Reditus Retorno." The lure leapt from her hand and as she suspected, sailed right across the street and back onto Mitch's property and into the garage before sputtering out. Mac and the boys didn't notice.

Mitch was definitely somewhere in that house.

She pulled the phone back from her ear and called her dad.

"Hello, Millie," Hank said.

"Dad, real quick. You did say you worked on Perry's and Mitch's houses, right, and they helped with ours?"

"Yes, I did."

"You remember anything specific about Mitch's house? Anything unique or odd?"

"Um...um. Let me think. This was a while back."

"Take your time." Millie didn't mean it. There was a killer to be caught in that house. *Hurry up, Dad.*

"Um..."

"I know Mitch was into hunting. Did he have a

special place built to store his guns or anything like that?" Millie asked.

"Oh yes, that's it. He had me make him a gun cabinet and some shelving too, except he wanted it in for his secret stash, he said. I think he only told Perry and me about it. He has a prepper stash room in a sub-basement that can be accessed in his basement! That was it!"

"What is a prepper stash, Dad?"

"Oh, you know your uncle Kenny has one. A secret room underground stocked with food and supplies in case the apocalypse comes or nuclear war something like that."

"Of course, Uncle Kenny has one! Thanks, Dad."

"You bet, buh bye."

"Dad for the win." Millie walked back across the street and back to the garage.

"We are just going to canvass the area and put out an APB with Mitch's description. Hopefully we will find him. At least, we have Rachel." Mac walked to meet Millie at the edge of the garage.

"No need to do that. There is still one more place we haven't looked."

CHAPTER THIRTY-FOUR

This time Vince had four more members of the GPD to help in the search in the basement for the entrance to the sub-basement and so-called prepper stash. Eight people total searching for one large man. The basement was fully furnished with a slate pool table, a full bar, and even a skee-ball machine. Mac was extremely jealous.

"Of course, the greatest basement ever is owned by a crazy doomsday prepper." Mac poked the walls with his cane. He even went over to a bookcase and started to pull the books out to open a secret passage. That didn't work.

"Tear it all apart like the firemen do in a fire, people. We need to find this guy. The entrance has to be somewhere."

The cops, undercover witch, and former cop scoured the basement for the murderer. They took down framed movie posters, moved a Jurassic Park pinball machine. They turned the faucets on and off in the bathroom. Lots of different things.

No progress.

"I think I found something." A uniformed female police officer, brunette with a tightly-pulled ponytail, pointed to the floor behind the bar.

"How cool would it be if one of the taps opened the secret entrance? I bet you it's the Miller Lite tapper!" Mac yelled.

"Must you be so childish, Mac?" Vince shook his head and walked over to the bar. All seven of them did as if gathering to take a shot.

"Look, there is a handle on the floor."

"Could be where he keeps the kegs. This is a fancy house," Mac said.

"Go ahead and open it," Vince commanded.

The young policewoman grabbed the handle and immediately jolted backward and hit the bottles along the back wall.

"Oh shit. It's electrified. Is she okay?" Vince put his hands on his head.

Bermudez jumped over the bar and checked her pulse. "She will be okay. Just gave her a jolt. She should wake up soon."

"Anybody have electric or thick leather gloves?" Mac noted.

"We could just cut the power, right?" another officer said.

"Doubt it. He probably has a generator down there. The point of a prepper stash is to be like a mini-home," Millie said.

"Well, now what the hell do we do?" Vince asked.

"Wait him out, but he could be down there for a long time!" Mac walked all the way over to the pool table on the other side of the basement and rolled the eight ball around.

Millie walked over to Mac.

"Mac, I could easily break through that floor. You just have to get everyone back upstairs."

"How?"

"A powerful spell, of course. Just get everyone out."

"I mean, how do I get everyone upstairs?" Mac asked.

"I don't know. Figure it out, hero cop."

"On it. Hey, Vince! Let's get back upstairs. I think I know a way to get in. Everybody has to come upstairs, though!"

"We have to get her looked at by the paramedics anyway. Looks like he holed up himself in there. Can't wait to hear your ingenious plan." Vince helped

Bermudez carry the brunette cop upstairs. The other three cops followed.

Mac winked at Millie.

Mac followed the parade of cops back up the stairs.

CHAPTER THIRTY-FIVE

Millie pulled her wand out of her jacket pocket. The basement was clear.

She walked back behind the bar and took a deep breath then aimed her wand at the floor handle.

"Repulse!" Millie shielded her face. The concussive blast from her wand tore into the cement floor and reinforced steel door. Sparks flew as the wiring for the electrified handle came loose.

"What the hell?" a deep male voice bellowed from below her.

"Mitch, come out. Rachel confessed!" Millie held her wand at the hole in the basement floor. She dared to take a few steps forward. Her heart beat faster. Even though she knew she could easily handle the supposed beefcake Mac spoke of.

"You don't have anything on me!" Mitch yelled.

A small object flew out from the prepper bunker.

A flash of light.

A deafening pop!

Mille fell onto her back. She couldn't see anything.

MAC AND VINCE heard a crash and then the loud bang.

"Where's Millie?" Vince asked Mac.

"That sounded like a flashbang." Mac dropped his cane and ran back down the stairs. Vince followed. Both had their firearms at the ready.

They ran down the stairs and looked at the bar on the right side of the basement.

There he stood. Mitch Halliburton holding his hunter's rifle like he was a damn Navy Seal. He fired a shot at Mac and Vince from behind the bar. The bullet smacked up against the wall right next to Mac's head.

"Mac, get down!" Vince yelled. His brother fired a shot back at Mitch. Mitch ducked behind the bar. Mac ducked down.

"Let's get to the pool table. It's across from the bar and will give us some room. Jesus Christ. I hope Millie is okay. I will shoot at him to cover our movement. Go!" Mac fired two shots from his .38 at the bar. Mitch must have still crouched behind the bar.

Vince ran to the pool table. Mac stayed back. He had no intention of going to the pool table, not with Millie somewhere near a cold-blooded monster like Halliburton.

"Mac! Get over here! What are you doing?" Vince yelled.

"Vincey, give me some suppressing fire."

Mitch popped back up and shot at Mac still near the bottom of the stairs. He missed at his feet. Mac rolled toward the bar but was still far away and exposed to more shots from the bloodthirsty hunter.

Vince shot three more shots at Mitch, who again took cover behind the bar.

"Do you have a plan besides rolling around on the carpet, Mac?" Vince yelled.

———

MILLIE RUBBED her eyes from her supine position behind the bar. She'd lost her wand somewhere in the rubble from her concussive spell. She regained partial vision and hearing. Her ears recovered but then were subject to more abuse from gunshots at different parts of the basement.

"Don't you go anywhere, little lady." Mitch pointed his rifle at her.

Millie shook her head and moved her hands around to feel for her wand.

"Get up!" Mitch dropped his rifle and pulled a large silver handgun from his back.

Son of a bitch. Millie stood up.

Mitch grabbed her. He was powerful. His muscles pressed against her neck and chest.

"I have your girlfriend back here! Let me out of here or she dies. Simple as that."

Millie gagged as he pulled her up and literally held her hostage from behind the bar.

"Don't think so." Mac popped up from in front of the bar and shot Mitch in his massive bicep. Blood spattered on Millie's face. Mitch let her go. Millie dove over the bar to safety.

"You are okay, right?" Mac wiped some of the blood off her face.

Vince, Bermudez, and the rest of the cops who joined in on the hunt all converged to the bar.

Mitch was just sitting on the broken glass and rubble. He held his bicep and stared blankly at the taps.

"Book him, Vince-O," Mac said with his arm around Millie. He slipped her wand under her armpit.

She felt safe in Mac's arms and didn't move her right arm to hold the wand in place.

CHAPTER THIRTY-SIX

Mac and Millie eagerly awaited Vince, who finally walked into the Geneva Police department break room.

"Mitch confessed. He just seemed like a broken man. He and Rachel were being blackmailed and manipulated by Perry. Perry wanted to both torture them and keep them separate after his corporate spy aka amateur PI Devlin Hanks caught Mitch and Rachel together. Perry had suspected Rachel was cheating for years apparently, according to Mitch. However, Rachel's position as America's sweetheart morning show host prevented her from leaving Perry. A husband who committed suicide is a lot more sympathetic of a story than a divorce because of her infidelity with her husband's former best friend."

"It certainly is. Man, I actually really liked Rachel," Millie said.

"Did Mitch confess to killing Devlin?" Mac asked.

"He did. Perry never talked about Devlin, but Mitch said Devlin was an amateur. They figured out who he was after Rachel recognized him in front of Mitch's house one night."

"Why would Devlin still be employed by Perry if he'd had what he needed to get what he wanted from them?" Mac rubbed his chin.

"He wasn't hired by Perry at the time of his death. Mitch hired him and set him up. Killed him."

"Whoa." Millie shook her head in disbelief.

"Oh yes, and Jackson just called and found a pair of black gloves in Mitch's car. We are examining it for residue from the .38. Not that it matters, since he confessed but still. It will confirm he shot the gun then handed it off to Rachel."

"Anybody ever find Rachel's gloves?"

"Nope, she must have got rid of those in the toilet at the Potter House or something. Hey, how did you two know to go back to Rachel and get her to crack?" Vince cocked his head and twiddled his thumbs together.

"It was something she said while we were in the bathroom at the Potter House. She seemed angry and distraught that Perry had died. She let it slip that she was glad. Glad he was dead," Millie said.

"You didn't think to share that with me that night?" Vince asked.

"She was distraught and crying very hard into my shoulder. I passed it off as just emotional reaction. Then when you guys hit a wall or two with the investigation, I called Mac in to see if he could push Rachel into talking more and he did so, brilliantly, I might add."

"Impressive work. Well, I need some sleep. I haven't slept in like two straight days. Two and a half days?" Vince laughed.

"See you later, Vincey. Love ya." Mac hugged his brother.

"Why didn't you come up with us, Millie? Why did you stay down there? You almost got yourself killed." Vince couldn't help himself apparently.

"You are right. I should have just gone up with you guys, but I heard some rustling like he may open the door. Then he blew it open."

Vince paused for a second. "Whatever. Just go. Get out of here, you two lovebirds."

CHAPTER THIRTY-SEVEN

Mac and Millie made it to Mac's condo door. Exhausted. The two of them. Millie could feel it.

"Tonight on the broom was absolutely amazing. What else did I want to tell you?" Mac said.

"It was awesome. So glad you enjoyed it. Mac, I have something to talk to you about."

"Oh, I never gave you your Valentine!" Mac pulled out the small manila envelope from his pants pocket.

"What is this? Why are we still standing in the hallway?" Millie laughed.

"Open it up and see." Mac smiled.

Millie wanted to talk to him about New York and her new opportunity with Salem Bank. She opened the envelope. It was a key. A key to his place. She smiled but was also conflicted.

"Mac, this is wonderful. Thank you."

"I figured you should have a key and maybe even think about, I don't know, being roommates or something like that? I love it here in Geneva and I love you. Why don't you open the door?"

Shoot. He loves it here. Mille sighed.

"Uh-oh, what is the matter?" Mac asked.

"I know you love it here. It is just that Salem Bank offered me a huge promotion, but I have to move to upstate New York and, well, I am seriously considering it. I keep going back and forth."

Mac paused.

"Millie, anywhere with you is home. Whatever you decide to do is okay with me. I feel at home with you, whether it's on a broom, on a murder case, or on top of my bed. Well, especially on top of my bed."

Millie laughed hard.

"Thank you for you being you, Mac O'Malley. I feel at home with you too."

"Besides, I am a writer now. I can write anywhere. I am also a writer who has never finished a manuscript, so there's that too."

Millie put her key in the door then gave her lover a proper Valentine's kiss.

THE END

THE SWEDISH DAYS SWINDLE: A MAC AND MILLIE MYSTERY BOOK 3

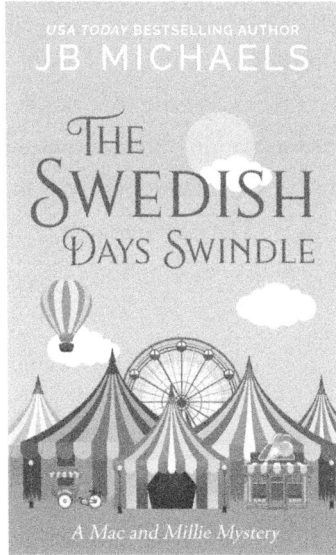

PREORDER NOW! It is Summertime in Geneva and the living's easy.

The Dying is also easy. Too easy.

Millie and Mac return to Third street to enjoy the simmering season's marquis event, Swedish Days.

Will our dynamic duo get to enjoy this Geneva event?

Or, will the day's fun lessen with murderous detriment?

At this point, you know the answer.

When a body bobs in the Fox River, Mac and Millie set aside their date to help solve the case of the deathly swimmer. As they examine the body, multiple downtown Geneva businesses report theft of their daily earnings.

A coincidence? Perhaps.

The unique shopping, delectable ice cream snacks, carnival rides, and concert vibes do little to lessen the impact when someone dies. As the evening fireworks are set to kindle, the Geneva Chamber of Commerce falls victim to the Swedish Days Swindle.

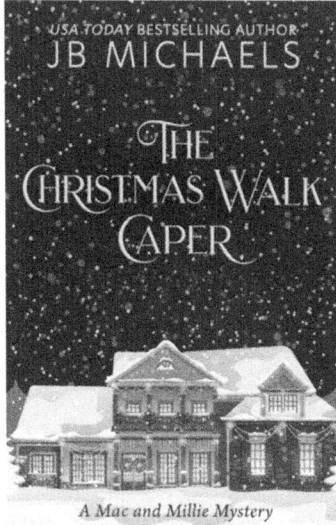

The book that started it all!

Add 'Catch a killer' to your Christmas to-do list!

In this delightful cozy mystery set in downtown Geneva,
Illinois, our sarcastic and savvy sleuths will seek justice for
the untimely death of the owner of the beloved and
charming retail mansion: The Tiny Wanderer.

"Millie has requested that I formally query you for your opinion of this crazy couple days in February in the form of a book review. So please leave a review of "The Valentine Dine or Die" We thank you very much. Also please my follow my buddy JB to keep in touch with him.

JB Michaels on Facebook!

JB on Amazon!

JB on Twitter!

JB on Instagram!

MAC, NON-WRITER AND RETIRED
CHICAGO COP.

PROLOGUE

"Stand together, men!" The battle-hardened legionary barked a desperate order.

The devastation surrounding the few soldiers struck fear into their brave hearts. Their brothers-in-arms once full of life and vigor, now lay dead in a most peculiar, inexplicable fashion.

"Shields at the ready! Let it come. We'll push it back together. Togeth—"

A thumping bass sounded once again. Though the sky painted a gloomy gray over the land, the source of this thunder was no storm.

Sweat poured from their helmets. Heavy gasps gave way to controlled breaths. The soldiers packed themselves into a square. Calloused hands gripped hilts of the devastatingly effective short sword—the gladius. Their visibility low, only the small space between their shields showed the danger that charged them. The force that killed their friends. Their fellow men of the mightiest empire the world had ever known —the toughest men born from the blood of their ancestors with the mission to spread the glory of Rome fell in great numbers this day. The remaining thoughts of their homes, their families, their futures, fell to the wayside as the need to survive prevailed.

The rumble of a beast's massive feet moved closer and closer.

"Stand ready, men! Get ready to push it back!"

The loud, guttural roar of the monster muted the centurion's commands and words of encouragement.

"Hold! Iehova be with us!"

CHAPTER ONE

Magnus Vicillius looked out onto the shoreline from the small rowboat powered by men in his charge. The gray sky and the cool temperature did little to welcome the warrior to Britannia. The temperature of the air served as harsh reminder of the wear on his body serving twenty years for SPQR. The Senate and the People of Rome relied on his service to maintain and strengthen the empire.

The neck of the muscular centurion ached. He hurt it pushing a battering ram into the walls of a Germanic fort.

There were many other scars that riddled his back. The barbarians sent out their women in the night to assassinate him and the other officers. He woke upon the first slash of many. Her wild demeanor nearly killed him. Magnus gained the advantage quickly, but his sleepy state caused him much grief. He rarely slept from that night forward. The incident proved his closest brush with death. No battle or bloody skirmishes with men bigger and stronger than he were as dangerous.

Still, Magnus neared the end of his term. In just five short years, he would receive the land promised to him and be able to live peacefully. Away from the frontiers filled with uncertainty and danger.

His reputation preceded him. A greeting party waited for him.

His men jumped from the rowboat into the shallows and pushed the boat up to the beach.

"Greetings, Magnus. Governor Gricola requests your presence immediately." A man dressed in gray robes surrounded by four soldiers looked deadly serious.

"Take me to him." Magnus, in full centurion regalia—full metal breastplate, his large belt which held Marius's mule, his centurion-class helmet with the crimson crest of hair— stepped onto the beach of dismal Britannia. His sandal-boots sank into the wet sand.

GOVERNOR GRICOLA RUBBED his hands on the robe covering his knees. "I sent them past the wall to attempt a peaceful conversion. They have yet to return. I sent for you to investigate and retrieve these men. I assure you I gave them orders to escort the missionary and march on peace and not conquest."

Magnus stood in front of the governor with his helmet under his arm. "The tribes in Caledonia historically don't take kindly to Roman legions marching onto their land no matter the mission."

"Of course, Vicillius. I wouldn't have sent them had I not sent scouts to procure a meeting with a tribal leader who sought knowledge of Iehova or Yeshua or whichever nomenclature they use. Of course, it would be in my best interest to bring Constantine's god to the frontier."

"I shall march with my men upon first light."

"No more time should be wasted. I'd hoped they would return in the time it took for the message to reach Rome. Alas, they have yet to return."

"I assure you, my men will find out what happened to them, Governor." Magnus stood tall in the lavish, intricate, wood-carved sitting room of the governor's villa.

"That is why I requested you, Magnus. You shall have the full complement of my local auxiliaries manning Hadrian's wall, if you please."

"Though I appreciate the gesture, we'd better not stir up the tribes with another larger force beyond the walls. If we need the might of your forces, I shall send my best messenger for their assistance."

"Remember, Magnus. There is a reason we built the wall. Please come back." The governor stood from his chair and nodded to Magnus.

The centurion didn't know if Gricola's plea was genuine. He'd just admitted that he sent the troop to help convert the pagans of the North to gain favor with the emperor. Over the years, Magnus realized that rarely were the intentions of the patricians in power purely selfless.

"I appreciate your concern for the finest soldiers of the empire. We will be back, Governor."

39

CHAPTER TWO

The next couple days were spent marching northwest to the walls. Magnus's force of one hundred men were more than up to the task, having quelled barbaric rebellions in Gaul and in the hinterlands of the Germanic forests. The battles of their storied pasts would serve them well in the wilds of Caledonia among the Picts and other tribes that lay stubborn claim to the northern section of Britannia. They made camp at Hadrian's Wall, about a day's march south of the unmanned Antonine wall and the last built physical barrier between Roman Britain and Caledonia.

Magnus removed his helmet and rubbed his scalp. "Tiberius, I want to take three men over this wall and possibly the old Antonine wall. I will accompany them. I need to know what happened, and we mustn't alarm the native tribes with a full century marching into their territory. You must stay with the rest of the legionaries here. I will need horses."

"Very well, Magnus. How will you know where to look for the missing?" Tiberius asked.

"The governor mentioned a tribal leader who sought knowledge of the Christian god. Upon first light, I will ask the auxiliaries who the tribal leader is and find him." Magnus sat on his blanket in the comfort of his tent.

"You speak of the Christian god as if he isn't yours to worship, Magnus. It would be wise not to use such casual jargon when speaking of Yeshua. Constantinius II is quite the believer in his father's converted belief. Many of the men believe, and I, myself, have grown quite fond of the message considering I have been digging ditches, building walls, bridges, aqueducts, and fighting for the empire the last twenty-four years with nary a sign from the gods that I am worthy of their dominion."

"Tiberius, I am aware of the men's predilection towards the Christian god. I must say I am unaware of your own thoughts of faith. I am Christian outwardly. We must be. It is our charge to be so. Privately, in my heart, I doubt that one man possessed such qualities to subsume and rule over the traditional Roman pantheon. My family gave tribute to the gods my whole life. I find it hard to break such tradition and belief at the request of the emperor."

"Yet you are a centurion, a valued leader of the most powerful army the world has ever known." Tiberius shook his head in frustration.

"I do and say what I must to maintain my position. Unlike you, I have five more years to go before I am granted citizenship. Now, if you would take your leave of my tent. I need rest. Who knows what awaits us beyond the wall?"

"Very well, Magnus. I shall see to it that you have your horses at first light. Any specific men you want on your sojourn?"

"No one specific. You pick. I need rest, Tiberius. Go."

40

CHAPTER THREE

The sun rose over the green land of Britannia. Magnus decided to wear his chest armor and carry Marius's mule, his tool bag, but would leave the rest of the armor in camp. For this jaunt over the wall, he favored speed and stealth over the usual brute force. He left his tent and waited for Tiberius with his men and horses. They were a few meters away.

"Your full armor will not be necessary. I would suggest taking blankets from my tent and using them as robes. I prefer us to go in quickly and commence with the investigation with as little disruption and attention drawn to us," Magnus barked.

"Meet your men, Magnus." Tiberius pointed to the trio from left to right. "Brayden, Romanus, and Cassius, three of the finest legionaries our century offers, and four black horses per your request."

The gray of Tiberius's hair was accentuated in the dawn's light. He looked older in the mornings. Magnus wondered if he looked as old to these young legionaries.

"Very well, men. I expect Tiberius has brought you up to speed. We must move with haste and stealth. Upon our exit through the gatehouse, we will ask the local auxiliaries where to find the tribal leader who asked to learn more of Yeshua." Magnus mounted his horse.

The three soldiers grabbed blankets and twine from Magnus's tent and made their shrouds from the dark blue blankets.

"Send Romanus back. He is the lightest on the horse with any news of emergency. The other two should be strong enough to provide substantial defense until the rest of the century can join you." Tiberius patted the neck of Magnus's horse.

"We shall hopefully return before the afternoon, Tiberius." Magnus turned his horse and rode away to the gatehouse walls. The soldiers three followed suit, barely securing their makeshift robes over their chest armor.

THE AUXILIARIES MANNING the wall looked disheveled and dirty. Not the ideal Roman soldier. The frontier and fringe units often didn't utilize the level of discipline and care that the fighting legions did.

"Sir, how may we be of assistance?" a soldier yelled from above them on the earthen and stone wall's gatehouse.

"We are requesting to get through to Caledonia. We have business to attend to. We also need to know the name of the chieftain, he who requested to know more of Yeshua."

"Aye, not a he, sir. A she."

"I beg your pardon." Magnus kept his frustration invisible, hoping he didn't hear him correctly.

"I said the chieftain is female, sir. A she, as it were. Her name is Michaela, and her tribe's village lies just over the first hill you see to the southwest. She commands the respect of the other tribes and is trusted to guard from any Roman intrusion."

"A woman?" Magnus pressed.

His horse neighed, urging him to move forward. Flashes of his near-death experience at the hands of a woman bothered him.

"Yes, a queen like Boudicca."

"Very well. Open the gate. I shall request an audience with this Michaela."

For young adults and up! The unique and thrilling adventures of Bud Hutchins, Maeve, and Ivy. They battle classic Hollywood monsters, avenge the dead, and save the world. Often. All the time actually.

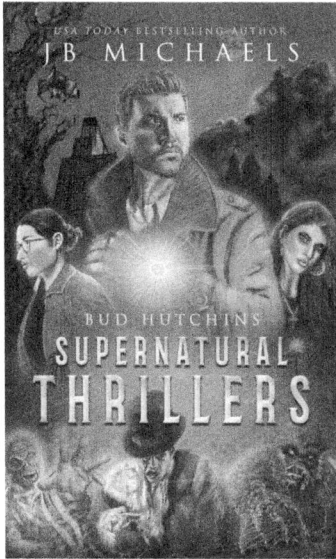

Battle Monsters. Avenge the dead. Join the Order!

ALSO BY JB MICHAELS

The Tannenbaum Tailors series- An incredible world in miniature. Mutli-Award-winners. Bestellers.

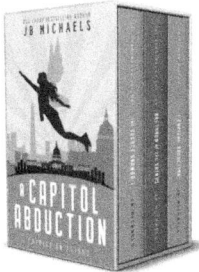

The Viking Throne! Experience the visceral thrills of "Taken" but on the high seas!

.

Made in the USA
Monee, IL
12 November 2021